THE KINGSNAKE IN THE SUN

A N O V E L

JOHN DE HERRERA

ALIPES
PRESS

Library of Congress Control Number: 2006921513
ISBN: 978-0-9778349-8-3

Published by Alipes Press

www.alipespress.com

P O Box 5888, Santa Barbara, CA 93108

Design/production by Margaret Dodd, Studio K Communication Arts
Printed in the United States of America by McNaughton & Gunn

to an actress

"We're not even allowed to talk about the truth, really...." So opens the rambling narrative of *The Kingsnake in the Sun*. Every generation has its *Huckleberry Finn,* and its *Catcher in the Rye*. In Jack Gaines, southern California surfer, we find a protagonist for a new generation to voice its concerns in this coming-of-age story—the latest in a long and rich literary genre of first-person narratives. Interweaving the mundane and the profound, the narrator explores the multiple tracks of youth journeying to find itself.

THE KINGSNAKE IN THE SUN

1

We're not even allowed to talk about the truth, really. And it's so unpleasant most of us wouldn't want to anyway. That's what *The Catcher in the Rye* is all about. Phoniness is the stuff everyone's doing while avoiding the truth. And at some point you have to accept not being able to talk about it, and join in the game, or if you balk too long, you end up depressed as hell and in a hospital. I was one of the ones who ended up in a hospital. If you want to hear about it, I'll tell you. In a way it's like the poem *The Rhyme of the Ancient Mariner*: "…that agony returns:/ And till my ghastly tale is told…." That's the way I feel about it sometimes, like I have to tell about it.

I guess I should start by saying that I read a lot growing up. I always saw reading books as hunting for treasure. But not many novels though, I always thought fiction was a waste of time when you could be reading about *reality*. I was assigned to read *The Catcher in the Rye* in junior high just like everyone. I never did. I got an F on the book report. The teacher who assigned it kept me after one day and asked why I hadn't read it. He was one of those guys with greasy hair, thick glasses, and big, slow, watery eyes.

I didn't listen to anything he was trying to tell me, and the next day I was on the way home from a hike when I saw a book in the road. As I was getting closer I thought about it maybe being *that book*. Closer up I saw the cover was missing. I got to it and there it was spelled out in black and white on the crinkled-up title page. The day before, having the teacher ask why I hadn't read it, and seeing it there in the road—I didn't know what to think. I remember I got mad in a way and what I did next was kind of weird but, looking back, maybe was kind of natural. I had to take a leak. So I picked it up like it was something dead, threw it over some bushes, went back there and took a leak on it. It was one of those long leaks too. Just soaked the thing. That might've been *that*, but then I saw it again the next night.

I was walking out of the market down the street from my house, turned the corner and bumped into this girl. I'd just bought some Cracker Jacks and was digging through the box looking for the prize when we both came around the corner and bumped. My Cracker Jacks flew and she spilled her purse. There were lipsticks, make-ups and stuff all over. I knelt down to help pick it up and there a couple feet away was the book. I handed it to her. One of the last things she picked up was the prize from my Cracker Jacks. "I think this is yours," she said. She was older than I was, like in twelfth grade. She was hot. I remember she was wearing a hat—a bowler—and her smooth brown bangs were flush down along her cheeks. She said Thanks and took off. I remember the prize was one of those little magnifying glasses you could use to burn your initials in stuff.

That was the last I saw or heard of it for years. Then I moved up to Santa Barbara to work for my dad—he owns a pharmacy. I moved because life down in Los Angeles started to get to me. My friends started to get on my nerves. We all grew up surfing and hanging out down at the beach. We talked the same, got drunk at the same parties, got in little squabbles, all that. But it started to seem like I couldn't shoot the shit the same as I used to. And even when I did, sometimes I felt like I was acting. I once read how patterns of thought get going in cliques and how it's tough to bust through them, and that's why some people never change, because the people they hang with don't. My dad mentioned he could use some help, so I moved.

I looked for a place to live for about a week. I wanted a place good for writing because I was working on a book of my own. It's a story about a cowboy—a Drifter—and how he gets a job as care-taker of a mansion, and how it turns out to be haunted by a Ghost Lady. I made it into a screenplay, but nobody wanted it. I got it into the hands of an agent for a big agency, and got rejected. That was another reason I moved, my brilliant script got turned down. I had talked it up pretty good while I was working on it too.

Before I moved I had a place lined up in case I didn't find anything better, but I checked the paper one last time and found a new ad about some rustic house on a mountainside. I called the number and got the answering machine. I left a message the first time, then hung up every other time until a girl answered. Before she gave directions she asked if I smoked or used drugs. I said No to both. I'll only smoke cigarettes if I've had a few beers at a party or wedding or something, and I hadn't smoked pot for a while. I told her I'd stop by after work.

The house was on Mountain Drive above Montecito. I drove up along the tree-lined roads, with all the mansion front gates, rolling lawns, manicured gardens. She said to look for an old driveway next to a bunch of mailboxes. I found it. The driveway was barely a driveway, more pothole than asphalt. I wheeled up the thing and came to the house. It was old too.

Set on an outcropping, the yard had a small deck, and from it was an incredible view—over Montecito, over downtown Santa

Barbara, the harbor, the ocean, the islands across the channel. You could see the coast from Isla Vista to down past Summerland. You could see a handful of oil derricks in the channel—which you'd think would ruin it, but they kind of added a depth of view to the ocean between the islands and the shore. At night they lit up and looked like little crystal ships, sometimes with a visible flame.

The house was custom—two-story-high ceilings, huge rough-hewn beams, Spanish tile floors. It's known in the neighborhood as the Castle. I found that out one morning waiting for a ride to work. I was at the foot of the driveway when a lady came along walking her two Irish setters. They ran over, sniffing and wagging their tails. The lady asked if I was new to the neighborhood, I said Yeah and pointed to where I lived. "Oh, the Castle," she said.

"Whaddaya mean?"

"Oh, there's a book about it. Back in the 60s they used to have parties there. The owners hosted a wine festival put on by artists of the area. Later, a record producer owned it. Hendrix and Joplin used to hang out there."

"Hendrix hung out there?"

"Yeah. The Doors once played a party right over on Coyote Road too."

"Wow. Were you around then?"

"Oh, no. My husband and I've only been here a few years. But I did some research when we first moved in," she said. "Welcome to the neighborhood."

Later that night after work, I cracked some beers, dug through CD's, and cranked Hendrix and Doors in front of the fireplace. Oh, and the fireplace there—it was *huge*. It was neat too because there were bits of graffiti carved all over the rock that made up the hearth and mantle. Most had been carved a while ago, all covered with smoke soot. I was always looking for a Jimi or Janis or Jim carved somewhere. There was a big M-O-T-H-E-R carved right in the middle of the mantle. The friends who came up to visit, I always told them Morrison did that one.

There was another carving I found that cracked me up—a peace sign, a plus sign, a heart, an equals sign, and a zero. Peace plus love equals zero—or nothingness. I pictured some guy all stoned back in the 60s or 70s carving it and thinking that that was *It*—which it probably is in some way.

*

I'd been living there at the Castle for about a month, when one weekend I was sitting on my bed reading *Rolling Stone*. There was an interview with an actress I was crazy about and it mentioned how much she loved *The Catcher in the Rye*. I thought about going out and getting it so I'd have something for conversation if I ever met her.

I'm sitting there daydreaming about her, when there's a knock on the front door. I answer it and it's the guy who'd moved out of the room I'd moved into. He'd stopped to check for messages or mail. I asked a few questions about the place, and as he was leaving he saw my skateboard and asked, "You been over to the Tea Gardens?"

"No. What's that?"

"There's a place down the road, an old abandoned property you can skate. It's got some pretty big bowls."

"Why do they call it the Tea Gardens?"

"Back in the 20s some lady had the mountainside landscaped

as a place to drink her morning tea. She was really into goldfish and imported them from around the world, so there's all these rad empty bowls to skate."

"Awesome."

"Just hop the gate and follow the trail, but be careful, the sheriff goes up there. You can get busted."

He left, and a little later I skated down to check it out. There was a big old iron gate set in a wall of sandstone blocks. I climbed over and went up the trail that led back into the property. A walkway led through a forest of different types of trees and overgrown hedges. The spiders were having a field day, there were giant webs all over.

The guy said to look for a line of oak trees. I went up along it and found the thing. It was a huge concrete bowl perfect for skating. It must've really been something back when it was built. There were big sandstone vases, cracked and crumbling, lining elaborate brickwork, and colorful tiles all along the edge. Instead of skating right then, I explored.

The path meandered along the steep hillsides all the way to the top. There, the property was a terrace with high sandstone arches and a view more incredible than the one from the Castle—which you could actually see down below, a couple ridges over.

There was a fountain and pond at the arches, and from them ran tributaries emptying into ponds that got bigger and bigger down the mountainside until they ended up in the one huge bowl at the bottom, the one you could skate.

No one was around that day. It was a gnarly little drop. Once I got it wired, found where all the smooth transitions were, I had a blast. After a while, I sat up on the edge to take a break and daydream about that actress. I looked out over the bowl. Even though it was huge, it was covered with graffiti—all kinds of surfing logos, skating logos, Fuck This, Fuck That, and Fuck Yous. Typical. I sat there and then for the heck of it let my board roll down into the bowl. It dropped to the bottom, shot up the other side, hit a pebble or crack, and flipped over. It slid back down a bit and stopped. I looked over for a second and then saw it, graffiti in the same colors as the cover—*The Catcher in the Rye*.

Just reading the stuff about the actress and how much she loved it, and remembering the stuff from when I was in junior high—I was pretty anxious to read it at that point.

*

Holden Caulfield is a crack-up! He's awesome. How great would it be to hang out with Holden for the day?! Back when I was his age, in my teens, I made up my mind I wasn't going to pretend at knowing it all. That was going to be my *knowing it all*—knowing I *didn't* know it all. I was afraid of losing a sense of wonder, and I wanted to be free to say, "I don't know." Which I guess is similar to not wanting to deal with phoniness.

Maybe Caulfield and I were the same in some ways, but there were way more differences. When I was young, we used to race Big Wheels and skateboards down the hills of our neighborhood. We used to have demolition derbies, and I was good at wiping other kids out. I took stuff out on kids in a way I don't think Caulfield would have. I threw mud in the eyes of this kid once. I said mean things. Most of it was before I knew better, and in my own defense, I have to say there were times when I helped, got kids included if they were left out, stuff like that. I was bad, but I wasn't all bad. Also, back then, for about a year I was a terror with a pellet gun. It was birds only. There was a grove of oak trees behind the high school. It was like a bird depot, and friends and I used to sit there and nail one after the other. But all that ended the day I killed a squirrel passing through the trees in our backyard. He was fifteen, twenty feet up. I took a shot and he stopped. We stared at each other while I pumped the gun again. His stare is still vivid in my mind. Personified, it was like, "You're not gonna kill me are you, you asshole?" I put him in the sights and his stare seemed to go, "Don't do it—don't do it—*you asshole.*" I pulled the trigger, he hung on the branch a moment, eyes glazed, and he dropped. I still remember the sound made on the carpet of leaves as he hit and slid to a stop in a rustle. Besides bugs, that was the last time I killed something intentionally.

I used to steal constantly too. I used to be a major klepto. Every time I walked into a store I'd pocket something. I used to wander around bookstores quite a bit—I used to have my own library until I had to sell it for rent.

Another thing about Caulfield though is, he went through his madman stuff in the 40s. When he got all depressed, dealing with life, and went into a bar, there was Big Band music playing—Goodman, Gershwin. What if he looked up and instead of seeing Ernie at the piano, he saw Hendrix ripping a Stratocaster? With neon go-go girls writhing on top of guitar amps? Or if he heard groups from Led Zeppelin to Nirvana?

Adolescent madman stuff will always go on, but I wonder if it's really any different for each era. I mean, I remember when computers started to get big, and the Internet took off, and news, entertainment and advertising merged, and people would say things like, "It's never been like this—things are crazier than ever!" But is that true? Is the craziness different, or is it the same, only with newer, sleeker gadgets?

I grew up in the Santa Monica Mountains between the San Fernando Valley and Malibu. That's where we moved to after my mom and dad got divorced and she got remarried. I was about four years old. The one clear memory I have of my *biological* dad was from the last day I saw him. He picked up my older brother and me to take us for the day. He took us to Olvera Street, downtown. There were Spanish ladies dancing, and Spanish guys playing trumpets, guitars, violins. There were piñatas and trinkets all over the place, the smell of grilled beef, churros. At one point he said I could pick out a toy from a chest full of stuff. It was a little painted wooden horse. I used to carry it around everywhere, hop it along the furniture in passing.

After the divorce was final, my mom got remarried to the dad I have now—the pharmacist. I didn't always consider him my dad. When I was in the judge's chamber that day, I was old enough to know this new guy wasn't my real dad. I was the biggest little bastard back then. I used to hurt his feelings all the time. I cringe remembering. Once, when we stopped for dinner after work, I went into how sorry I was for being an idiot when I was younger. He told me it was the past, that I wasn't that bad, and to forget about it. When I asked about my biological dad, all he knew was that he seemed like a nice guy the couple times they'd met, and that he must've been too young to handle my mom and three kids.

When I asked my mom, all she ever said was that he was a drunk and wouldn't talk about him. My brother told about a night she got us out of bed, put us in the car and drove to a local bar. We waited there—I was asleep—until my dad came out drunk, a woman on each arm, before noticing us in the car.

15

What my granddad, my mom's dad, told me is pretty much what remains in my mind about my biological dad. He said he used to ride in rodeos, and that in the 50s he won Saddle-Bronc Class, State Champ at the Cow Palace in San Francisco. He said he loved us but couldn't settle down, and they ended up getting divorced. My granddad said he'd heard he'd died and wouldn't have been surprised with the way he lived. I had a dream where he was on a horse in a meadow, his face shadowed by his hat.

When my mom got remarried, there was my older brother, younger sister, two new brothers from my new dad, and myself. A couple years later another brother came along and *that's the way we became the Brady Bunch.* I remember watching reruns of that show and how it normalized what I thought, like, Oh, we're a Brady Bunch–type family.

That's really all you need to know about my family. I could go on, about camping trips, going to the beach most weekends after church—all that. But I don't want to drag them into this. In this case it's really true what they say, never judge a person by their relatives.

*

There're a couple other things to tell. When I was four, my brother and the baby-sitter used to watch reruns of old TV shows. I remember this one show with a pretty blonde girl in it, and one day I was going through a shoe box of my brother's stuff when I find a stack of bubble-gum cards—cards they'd put out of the show. I started flipping through them and separated the ones with the blonde girl from the rest. Then I came across one of just her. I got dizzy. I swear, an actual physical sensation occurred as I looked at it. I was crazy about her. I even got into a routine where

I'd go and just sit and stare at that card of her. I'd even kiss it.

There was another TV show they used to watch. The show was *Batman* but the thing that drove me wild was *Catwoman*. I always thought Batman was stupid for not getting around to kissing her. I was glued to the set when there was an episode with Catwoman on.

To sum up, kissing the girl's bubble-gum card and not knowing exactly what I wanted to do with Catwoman but knowing I wanted to do something, I have to say, I was crazy about females at an unusually young age—I mean, I got hassled by other guys in kindergarten for kissing girls.

But I did meet Catwoman. When I was living at the Castle there seemed to be some kind of bizarre coincidence going on all the time. Or one that took place over a couple of days, a week or something—like this one when I met Catwoman.

*

It started when I was going through a bookstore. I was on a lunch break in a sandwich shop, and they had a comic book section in the back. As a kid I never read comics. Some friends down the street had them. I knew all the heroes—Superman, Batman, Spiderman—but had never really read them. This one day though, I started going through this comic book section. The reason was because of what I was reading at the time. I was into the book they made about the series *The Power of Myth* with Joseph Campbell. And I'd already read through a lot of Jung, so I was well into the investigation of archetypal stuff.

I came across this comic titled *Catwoman*, and curious about how she'd be portrayed, I got it. Later that night, flipping through the channels on TV, I happened to land on an old episode of *Batman*—one with Catwoman. It's the one where she's trying to get hold of some golden cat statues.

The comic was one in a series of four, and for the rest of the week I tracked down the other three. Calling around to comic book stores, I found out a little about them.

There're different ages in comics. There's the Golden Age, when they first appeared in the 40s through the 50s. Then the Silver Age, from the 60s to 70s, and the Modern Age. A guy at one store knew everything—a comic book fiend. I asked questions like, what heroes were around in the Golden Age that are still around now, and how they've changed through the ages. I asked about Catwoman, and what's weird is that in the Golden Age, Batman *marries* Catwoman. They even have a kid, a girl who grows up to be the Huntress. Isn't that unreal? In the Golden Age, Batman and Catwoman get married. Archetypally it's pretty fascinating.

After getting the other three comics through the mail, that weekend I went back down to LA to work a parade. I had a job sometimes where I'd pull a cart along parade routes. It's an old surfer thing—some of the older guys figured out you could buy a cotton-candy maker, weld some carts together, and make a lot of cash selling stuff on the weekends.

The parade that day was in Brentwood. The crew who did parades, we all knew each other from school or surfing, hanging down at Rockbed. The parade started, we got out on the route, and I was doing horrible because I'd made the mistake of taking a couple hits off a joint that went around as we set up. I get all self-conscious when I get stoned. I mean when I first started getting stoned, I never did. But what usually took place when I got stoned, I'd go to the end of the route, pull the ice chest out from under the cart, sit down and watch the parade. I'd only end up selling stuff if people came over for something.

That day in Brentwood though, I was at the end, sitting there watching, when a kid came up to get a balloon. I got the color they wanted, turned around to hand it over, and there in the parade, up on the back seat of a convertible, was Catwoman. She was wearing a sundress and broad-brimmed hat. She had her arm around a disabled kid. There was a banner alongside the car for a charity. I felt like I had to say something.

In the center of that part of San Vicente, there's an island of grass with big old coral trees. At the very end of the route the cars in the parade were making a U-turn and coming up the street on the other side of the grass island. So I hauled my cart across the island quick—except not that quick, because I'd gotten stoned, which meant I hadn't been walking the route selling stuff, and my ice chest was full of cokes and heavy, and the cart wheels kept getting stuck in the grass. But I got to the other side and watched her car. I had no idea what to say. The guy driving didn't look like he'd slow down. I decided against waving for them to stop.

So the car's coming right at me, she's looking over at the parade, and within about twenty yards I call out. She turned towards me, raising her hand to the top of her hat as the brim blew up and we made eye contact. "I love you," I said. Her eyes stayed with mine as she passed within a few feet. She made a sexy little cat sound.

It turns out the four comics are already worth something. I was in another store not long ago and asked. They said the art and story line are good as far as comics go, and the whole set is worth something. The story line that runs through it is archetypal of course. For instance in the comic, Catwoman has a long-lost sister who's a nun, and when Catwoman's old pimp kidnaps her, she gets some shady character to teach her how to fight and knock guys out—except it ends up taking Batman to save the nun. It's all archetypal, just more refined.

I guess I should tell you how I even found out about archetypal stuff in the first place. What happened is, one night I met this lady, the Goddess Lady.

2

The first time I saw her I was spun-out on coffee. It was two or three in the morning and I was sitting in a donut shop facing a small parking lot and Ventura Boulevard. She pulled off Ventura in a green van and parked in front of the 7-Eleven next door. There were two large dogs riding with her, a German shepherd in the back and a black Lab, whose head stuck out the window, in the front. The parking lot was empty, the streets were empty, and being the only two people around, we made eye contact. It was real quick, just a second, before she blinked slowly, looking away. She was one of those females who are so hot it seemed like she had a light around her.

Her eyes were blue, her hair a shade between strawberry blond and auburn. It was fine, silky, and up in a bun. It had that smooth, shiny look silky hair gets when it's up in a bun. Her cheekbones were high, her nose small and slightly turned-up. Her lips were pink and fragile-looking, like a kid's—well-proportioned but delicate. And her chin was pointed, though still had a roundness—cute. Any make-up at all was eyeliner. She was really something. I was in shock as a matter of fact, and the only thoughts my mind allowed were of how I was going to get a word with her. She climbed out of her car. Small-breasted and slender, she was wearing a man's tank-top undershirt—no bra—light purple sweat pants, and white high-top tennis shoes. I watched her walk towards the 7-Eleven as I stood from my seat, my mind racing. I *had* to talk to her.

The reason I was there in the first place? Two or three in the morning, spun-out on coffee? I was a bum. I mean, not a *bum* bum—but a bum. I was twenty and just recently booted from the house. At the time, yeah, I thought the folks were jerks kicking me out, but looking back, all I was doing was running around, surfing all day, staying out all night and, being a bum. I had a job, but nothing saved.

I slept on friends' couches for a while, but if you've ever found yourself in that situation, you know how it gets old quick. And so, on nights the hospitality of friends needed to recharge, it was coffee and the smell of donuts.

But I had to talk to her, right? So what I did was, I walked outside, walked over to the phones on the wall and stood there, right in front of her van. She had good dogs, they didn't crowd the windshield and bark or anything. Besides the Lab poking his fat head out the window, trying to get a scent of me, they stayed seated. They just sat there looking at me like, "He might throw a pretty good stick."

I had no plan. She came out with a bag of dog food in one arm and a gallon of water in the other. We looked at each other. I smiled, she smiled, and I said, "Need some help?"

"No thanks, I got it." Her voice was sweet. A cheery tone, its pitch arced in a warm way with each phrase. The driver's side window was rolled down, she reached in with the water and set it on the seat. Right then I blurted, "Say, you wouldn't happen to have a quarter—would ya?" It was all I could think of. She opened her car door, set the dog food next to the dog, stood back upright, sized me up and said, "Sure." She climbed in and shut the door as I approached. She reached over to her ashtray, full of silver, and picked out a quarter. I held out my hand and she dropped it onto my palm. We made close-up eye contact. Her eyes were a deep blue, not an icy or powder blue. She was awesome—auburn, blue, and fair.

She smiled with a slight nod. I gave her door a soft knock with my knuckle, said Thanks, and turned towards the phones. I barely made a step, when from over my shoulder came, "Do you need a ride somewhere?"

Now, let me point out, I've always been an exceptional daydreamer, and most of the time I sat there smelling donuts, I daydreamed about a beautiful woman coming in and asking if I needed a place to stay. At that moment, there in front of me, was a dream come true! She didn't ask if I needed a place to stay exactly, but I could've gotten in her car, started up some talk, and taken it from there. But I didn't! I just said "Ah, that's all right, I only need to make a call—thanks though." It just came out of my mouth.

And so, one of the most beautiful women I'd ever seen, with her dogs, she drove away. I went back into the donut shop, sat down and grieved for the rest of the night that I didn't get in her car. That was the first time I saw her.

About four or five days later I was across the street from the 7-Eleven. I was at a burger place waiting for my boss. I had this job at the time doing door-to-door sales. We only worked from five-thirty to nine—that's how I got to surf all day and stay out all night.

So I'm sitting there out front eating, when I see her again. Same green van, same two dogs—it was her. She was cleaning her windshield at the gas station, and I didn't have a quarter to go over and pay her back with.

I watched her drive away again. I was bummed, she was hot. That was the second time I saw her.

*

In the following weeks I got a bit of my act together, rounded up enough cash for first and last, and became a renter for the first time. It was a room made from part of a garage, small and cheap, with its own bathroom. I was stoked.

The landlady was cool. Her name was Grace. She was in her forties, in good shape, green eyes and blonde hair. She'd been married twice, one of her ex-husbands always came around hoping to get back together. She was from the South, talked with a drawl, was into her horses—Talon and Sage—and it was part of my rent to feed them and clean the corral.

The house was in a part of the Santa Monicas I'd never explored too much. Zuma and the surf was ten minutes down the road. My sales job, which I then took with some seriousness, was over the hill in the valley, and I started classes at the local junior college. I was still living hand-to-mouth. Every dime that could be spent, still leaving a bed to crash on, was spent. But I was doing it on my own for the first time and it felt good. Life is ten times more romantic when you wake up to take a shower you paid for yourself.

*

A month or so had gone by since the stints in the donut shop. Classes were easy enough to get C's, and I was salesman-of-the-week a few times, which afforded me an old truck. Things were going pretty good, and it was a hot spring day when I came home from a morning surf. Out in the line-up I'd made plans with a buddy to meet over at his house to get stoned and shoot pool before the sales job. I dropped off my board and suit, and instead of hopping on the freeway, I decided to take Mulholland Highway all the way over.

It was really brilliant out—the sky almost wasn't there, only sun and sunlight. It was hot, but a springtime hot, not a summer-time hot. Animals—lizards, birds, squirrels—were all over the place, and everything was so green and intense I was actually going the speed limit taking it all in.

The Santa Monica Mountains and the Santa Ynez Mountains, the two ranges along the coast from Santa Barbara to Malibu, are the same. I call those two ranges, along with the Channel Islands, the Triangle of Paradise. It's that Mediterranean climate next to the ocean, a place where chaparral and oak meet the sea, a place with a lot of days where your skin is tickled by the breeze. Like if you were sitting around in a bathing suit, and it's not too cool, and it's not too warm, and there's a breeze, and it kind of tickles your skin—kind of womb-like I guess.

Anyway, I'm on my way over on Mulholland, passing Old Topanga Canyon Road, when she came around the turn. It was the green van I saw first. I hadn't thought about her in weeks—in my thoughts she'd become known as the Goddess Lady—but everything came back in a flash when I saw her up close at the wheel. I hesitated a second, then slammed the brakes, made a U-turn, and took off after her. I came back around the turn just in time to see her disappear around the first corner going up Old Topanga.

I catch up, she's in her car, I'm in mine, and I start figuring like mad. If I honk she'll think some crazy guy's following her. As we passed through the lower part of the canyon, alongside the creek, under the oak and sycamore, I tried to come up with something different, but besides plain running her off the road, there wasn't anything else to do. So I honk. And when I see her look back through her mirror, I put up my hand in a stop sign, mouth something like, "Wait a minute," and, to my worst fears, she speeds up—some crazy guy's following her!

I drive on in agony behind her as she glances back, as I try and somehow convey I'm not a crazy guy, and I just want to pay her back. Then a straightaway came up. I pulled over real quick, honked again while hopping out of the truck, jumped in the road, and made some body language like, "I just wanna give you your quarter back." I stood there watching her car drive away for the third time. It was horrible—but then—near the end of the straightaway—before a turn up the hill and out of sight—she pulled off onto the dirt shoulder. Dust flew up and I was off running towards her.

They'd just repaved that stretch of road. I was barefoot in a pair of surf trunks, and although the soles of my feet were leathery from going around without shoes, the road was really hot.

When I got up to her she had sunglasses on. Aviator-style, a dark purple that faded to violet at the bottom of the lens. I got face to face with her, standing back in the road some so she wouldn't feel threatened or anything. Everything was bright, vivid. She must've just washed her van, there was all this light coming off it. It was so bright that day it seemed like everything was shining. I stood there squinting, and started going into how she'd loaned me a quarter that night. Listening, she slid her glasses down her nose. Her eyes were amazing. A rich blue, the color of sky right after a rain—you almost had to make a conscious decision to look away, they were that beautiful. The next thing I knew she started laughing. I didn't realize it, but standing in the road there, I'd started doing a little jig—my feet were cooking! I asked her for her number.

Shooting pool back at my friend's, I was in a daze—the Goddess Lady—I had her number.

*

At the time I was in the habit of hiking this one mountain peak every afternoon. It's the one in Malibu Canyon with the cross on the top. You can see it over your right shoulder as you cross the bridge headed for the beach. My buddies and I just call it the Peak. When we were all together hanging out after a surf, looking for something to do, invariably one of us would throw out a, "We could hike the peak." That was usually me. It takes about an hour and a half to get to the top.

I can't remember, but either the boss called off sales or I blew them off for the night, so after playing pool, I went for a hike. I went along Malibu Creek, up through a connecting ravine, and then up onto the fire road. That was the first spot to take a breather. I was thinking about her like crazy.

I get into the thick of the hike, off the fire road and on up the next ravine. In a year with plenty of rain there's water. That day it was only a trickle in places. I start on up, and all of a sudden, from behind a bush, taking to flight, was a huge great horned owl. It scared me. To suddenly hear and see the beating, slapping wings of a large bird of prey take flight a couple yards away is pretty intense. I went over where he flew out from, expecting to find a half-eaten rabbit or something, but there was nothing there. I wondered if owls slept like that during the day. You never see owls in the day, always at dusk, or in your headlights at night, flying off the side of the road, or a silhouette of one on a power line.

The hike from that point, further up from where the owl was, gets steep. It's the south face. No one climbs that side, the side with the cliffs. It's pretty gnarly—a bunch of places you could die if you fell. The lower part of the hike mainly consisted of climbing dried waterfalls to dried pools. I go at it, and after a half-hour or so, I stop to take another breather. With all the endorphins, I was daydreaming like mad, looking out over the canyon, the winding of Piuma Road, and a wedge of the Santa Monica Bay visible through the crag. I was imagining how our first conversation would go, practiced some lines I might try.

Finished with the break, I turned around to see where I was going to continue climbing, and then I saw it. Spread out evenly across the top of a dried-up waterfall was a scarlet kingsnake. Crimson red, black, and white, about three feet long, it had just shed its skin and was in stark contrast to the dullish grey rock. It was just there, shining in the sun. It was dreamlike. Nature came together in color and form in that instant to become so beautiful that it was stunning. After a minute or two there was an impulse to get up there and catch it, but I didn't. It was too beautiful. Scarlet kingsnakes are rare too. In all my years hiking, I'd never seen one on my own. When I was about ten I'd seen one in an aquarium, in the garage of an older neighborhood guy who'd caught it. And back in school there were occasional stories, sightings from other guys, but that was the first one I'd ever discovered myself.

I finished hiking up to the cross—a big, whitewashed, wooden cross—which, we'd always heard, was up there as a memorial to a fireman who died in the line of duty.

*

I got home and called. Her phone rang and rang and I wondered if she'd given a fake number. Then the machine clicked on. After thinking I'd be smooth, I blanked, and hung up. Then I called back real quick to hear her voice again.

About a year or so before, I'd gotten in a habit of listening to people's voices. What happened was, one night a buddy and I were drinking beers, when he started talking about his girlfriend. They'd been going out and breaking up and making up for a while — they had that type of relationship — and he's talking about her and what she's doing wrong, when instead of listening to his words, I started hearing his voice. The tone of it throughout the sentences, it was like seeing color for the first time. I only heard voice, and the pitch and the emotion within it. I think it was the first time I heard the subtext to what a person was talking about, and about a week later I was flipping through a dictionary when I came across a word *cadence*. It's listed as the rising or falling in a voice or sound. For a while all I did was go around studying the cadences of people's voices. It didn't matter who I was talking to, or about what, I'd be listening to the cadence of their voice. I listened to it in the music I was into back then too, stuff on the radio. After that went on a while it got even worse when I started trying to figure out links between certain cadences and conversational metaphors. I don't listen like that now — sometimes though. Like listening to the Goddess Lady's voice on her machine. It was smooth, even, and although it didn't exactly have the cadence a lady can get when she's being sexy, like in commercials, it still made me horny.

I called her the next day. She answered, and none of my smooth talk seemed to do anything, nothing I said got the response I wanted. The only thing I remember about that first conversation, besides her talking to me the way an older sister would, was that she said something about me being this thing called a *puer*.

"Do you read much?" she asked.

"Yeah." She suggested some titles I might want to check out if I was interested.

If I was interested? She was so incredible, she reminded me of that actress in the movie *Ladyhawke*. Very serious and very beautiful all at once. I went to the library.

The books she mentioned over the phone that I jotted down were by this guy Carl Gustav Jung. I still have the page I jotted the stuff on. It's on a back page of one of my journals with an incorrect spelling of *Puer Aeternus* and the word *archetype*.

The next day at the library, I looked up Jung, books about Jungian psychology, and went straight to the index looking for that word *puer*.

*

She lived in Topanga Canyon. She was a house cleaner. She insisted that she cleaned space. Apparently she was really good at what she did because she *chose* who her clients were. She turned business away. After hanging out one day, we stopped at her place, she checked messages, and there was one from a lady who practically gave a resume of stuff like being a vegetarian, a volunteer, and who else she knew in the canyon, so she could be considered a client. When I heard it, I was like, "Who are you—the Tinkerbell of Topanga Canyon?"

"No," she said. "I just work hard at what I do, and to do that is important. But you're still too young to understand."

"No I'm not."

"Yes you are."

I was twenty, she was thirty, and summer was just starting.

*

The first time we made out, we started getting pretty hot and then she told me she'd been raped. From there on I made it a point of letting her let me know if she wanted to do anything besides just kissing.

The first time we did it, it was a weekend, and she was house-sitting. The house was a client's, way up above the canyon. From it you could see all the beach towns lining Santa Monica Bay, Palos Verdes, Catalina, and a couple other islands in the distance. I was sitting at the piano messing around. I can't play really, but I can make stuff up. I played violin when I was a kid. My teacher said I had an ear for music. I can play a guitar a little too.

We had plans to go down to the beach and run her dogs. I got up and turned around to see if she was ready to go, and there she was, watching me from this big black leather couch across the room. We looked at each other.

"Are you ready?"

"Yes."

The way she was looking at me and the way she said it, I went over to her, slipped my arm under her waist, brought her on her back with her hair spilling all over the pillows, and we started kissing like mad. Before when we got all hot like that, she had always left her panties on. She was going to have to let me know when she was ready. But this time I scooted them down a bit and she left them there. After another beat or two, I took them off. I set it up, she let me know it was all right, and we went all the way.

It was incredible. She was incredible. I hung on for as long as I could. It was hard not to let go with her though. Finished, lying there and calming down, she put her arms around me and started crying.

"What's wrong?"

"Nothing—I'm just happy. I never thought I'd be like this again. You healed me. Thank you for being patient."

"It wasn't easy, but you were worth the wait," I said. A few minutes later I asked if I could heal her again.

*

We saw each other a few times a week. We did most the normal stuff. We'd go to museums, bookstores, movies, the beach. We went to the animal shelter quite a bit too. She'd always volunteer to take a client's or neighbor's pet to get spayed or neutered. She was crazy about animals and their welfare. There was more than once we came across a dog or cat stranded or wandering around somewhere, and we'd take them to an animal shelter. There was more than once we stopped. She was crazy about animals.

I remember once I was going to meet her at the shelter in Agoura on my way to work, while she was getting some critter fixed. On the way, I'd stopped and picked a rose to have for her when we met up. I got there, she was busy talking to the vet, I was late, and I decided to leave it on her windshield with a note that I'd call later. Except as I was doing that, I noticed a couple petals were wilted at the tips. You know how when you pick a petal off a rose, or most any flower for that matter, that there's the color of the petal, and the colors that fade towards the hip? I thought that looked pretty, like a sunrise or sunset, so I took apart this rose, folded all the petals in a note of when to call, and put that on her windshield. It's not the most romantic thing you've ever heard, but what I'm saying is, I was in that mode—the mode where you're concerned whether a rose you picked is perfect or not.

*

She could really cook a meal too. And she was totally into all these natural foods. I remember the first thing she ever made for me was my favorite sandwich. She asked if she could make me something.

"Yeah sure," I said.

"What do you feel like?"

"Whatever's easiest." I was looking over the books she had on the shelves in her little den. She had a pretty good collection, a lot of stuff I'd never read.

"How was Prowst?" I asked. I pronounced his name wrong.

"It's pronounced Proost, I think," she said. "Pretty incredible insights found in that book."

She had a lot of Hemingway.

"You like Hemingway?"

"Yeah, do you like him?"

"I read *The Sun Also Rises*—it was pretty good. What's your favorite by him?"

"I like most of his work, as you can probably tell. I really enjoyed *A Moveable Feast*. It's a nonfiction narrative about him and other artists in France in the 20s. He really berates Fitzgerald."

"*Berates?*" I said.

"Puts him down."

I told her I'd read *The Great Gatsby* and thought it was good.

She had all of Salinger's books, but I didn't go into all *The Catcher in the Rye* stuff right then. I asked what she thought about it though. She loved it of course.

"Did you know Salinger was in World War II?" she asked.

"Was he?"

"Yeah," she said. "A lot of people don't know that, but he was in a couple of major battles in Germany. He also landed on one of the beaches at Normandy."

"Really?"

"He met Hemingway when he was there too," she said. "He was a little disenchanted though."

"Yeah? How come?"

"The story goes that Hemingway was arguing with some other GIs about the finer points of a Luger, and to prove his point, shot the head off a cat or chicken or something."

"You know what a Luger is?" I asked.

"It's the pistol most Germans used in the war, right?"

"Yeah. Why was Salinger disenchanted?"

"Hemingway and Salinger were just two different types of men," she said. "Salinger wasn't the type to shoot and kill something to prove a point."

She called me into the kitchen and there was a plump tuna and avocado sandwich—my favorite—sitting on the table. She could make an awesome boysenberry pie too, just the right ratio of crust and filling.

*

Once while having breakfast we decided to hurry and head up to the naval air station for the air show. It was my idea. I like seeing the fighter jets. I had to talk her into it a little, but when she saw how excited I started to get about it, she decided to go.

I remember it was an overcast morning along Pacific Coast Highway. I was all excited and was going kind of fast. I started talking about my favorite kinds of jets—which, I probably have to say, my all-time favorite is the F-16. Just because it's small compared to the F-14 and F-15, and the canopy is all view. Although the F-16 is called the Falcon, it's actually the F-14 Tomcat that's the most falciform. That's a word I found once, *falciform*. It means that signature form of a bird of prey descending to its target. Wings swept back, the F-14 looks most like that. That's the type they flew in the movie *Top Gun*.

"You should slow down a little," she said. "You're speeding."

"I have to. We gotta get up there. The parking's outta control."

"Suit yourself," she shrugged, and I kept going on about jets.

"As a kid my favorite was the F-4. Just the way it looked, the tips of the wings slanted up, the tail wings slanted down—it always looked so tough."

"Have you ever been in a plane?"

"A couple times, yeah."

"What did you think? How did it make you feel?" She was turned towards me with half her back on the side of the seat and half against the door, like she was in a booth talking to someone driving.

"I loved it. I love flying. If there's one thing I have to do, it's fly in a fighter jet."

We drove on a second and then she said, "You're a flying *puer*."

"Oh yeah? You mean there's different kinds?"

"Well, let's say some travel closer to the ground," she said.

"Hmm. Anyway, the F-18—"

"Homosexual men are really attracted to that type."

"*What*? Whaddaya mean? I don't even wanna know—"

"Why? Does it bother you to talk about homosexuals?"

"No, not really—well yeah, I guess, a little." Right then, we passed this big, dead raccoon in the middle of the road.

"Oh, we better get that out of the road," she said.

"What?"

"I mean we should get that raccoon out of the road." She was serious.

"C'mon."

"Right now I'm feeling like we should—"

"We can't. We're in a hurry."

"I think we should."

"Why?"

"Because, it will only take a minute. And it will put us somewhere else."

"Put us somewhere else? Whaddaya mean?"

"Fine," she said. "Forget it."

"OK. But what do you mean, 'It'll put us somewhere else?'" She sighed, and straightened up in her seat.

"C'mon, whaddaya mean?"

"There're times—if you take time out of your agenda for someone else—it alters your course in life. It's a form of prayer."

"A form of prayer?"

"Yeah."

"How so?"

"When most people pray, they pray for something they want to happen, right?"

"Yeah."

"Well, a lot of the time for something to happen, you have to be in the right place at the right time. So, taking time to commit a selfless act means you'll end up somewhere different at a different time. And maybe that will be the time and place your prayer is answered. That's all."

"Yeah, but that was roadkill—how's that—"

"Oh forget about it, I don't know what I was thinking."

Then I looked in my mirror, saw a motorcycle cop with lights on, and got handed a speeding ticket.

*

We were hanging out one day—her, myself, and her dogs. We were in a canyon having a picnic when she said she didn't think I could climb to the top of a rock formation in a certain amount of time. Actually I'd brought it up, I knew I could. I went up, climbing the gnarly parts of the face, showing off, and when I came back down out of the bushes—her dogs right behind—she looked at me a little starry-eyed.

"You're really good at that."

"I've spent so much time doing it I should be pretty good. Thanks."

"Why do you think you've spent so much time hiking and climbing?"

"I don't know."

"What do you get out of it?"

"Climbing up the face of a cliff, way up there, the rock warm under your feet, the breeze—that's when it really pays off. There's something almost mystical about it."

"*Really?*"

"There's something about height, about examining things from above, the clarity of looking down on something. Maybe that's what I like."

"Have you read any Jung yet?"

"Not really."

She was slightly disappointed.

"What is this *puer* thing anyway? What does that mean?"

"The *Puer Aeternus* and the *Puella Aeterna* are archetypes."

*

There're three main components to the psyche in Jungian theory. There's the Ego, the thing you use to deal and maneuver through reality with—the Unconscious, the part where everything that's gone on around you since you were born is stored—and the Collective Unconscious, the part full of all the stuff humankind's been through, through the ages.

If it was put into a metaphor, you could look at the collective unconscious as a riverbed, where the river is Time, and the riverbed is the sediment of change and experience. The sediment on top is the most recent stuff the river has brought—like say, the Industrial Revolution—the experience of living with machinery.

Another analogy for the psyche is the ocean, where the ego is a boat, the unconscious the ocean, and the sea depths the collective unconscious. Which kind of means, the deeper you go into your personal unconscious, the more collective experience becomes. For instance, way deep, from times of old, there is the collective experience of snakes, and if you happen upon one you're taken aback—or plain old freak out. Suddenly seeing a snake, you're seized with the collective experience, the human experience, of snakes. And if you go deeper into the collective experience, it starts to get biological. For instance, color. Everyone sees the color red as a warm color—it excites, it actually has a physiological effect on the body. Your heart rate increases, things dilate, whereas blue has the opposite effect—it's cool, it soothes.

Anyway, Jung studied folktales and mythologies, and he started to notice that some stories are common to cultures all around the world. Some of the stories are *archetypal*, and the figures who inhabit them are *archetypes*. The hero is the most universal archetype, you can find it in the mythologies and folktales of any culture. It's the archetype of someone set on a journey who has to go through different kinds of trials to bring back gold from the forest to save the village, or win the princess's love. Joseph Campbell elaborated on it all in his books.

As far as the archetypal structure of the human psyche—it's universal. The same way the human form is universal—head, arms, legs, fingers, toes—we've all got the hero archetype in our minds. And guys have the archetype of the ideal woman, and women have the archetype of the ideal man—and we all have a Shadow archetype—the one that embodies everything we think evil is. The hero, the opposite sex, and the devil are archetypes of every human psyche.

The movie *Batman* is a good example of archetypal stuff. Take that movie and put it up against the folktale of the knight who slays the dragon to save the maiden. Batman is the knight, the Joker is the dragon, and Vicki Vale is the maiden. The Knight–Dragon–Fair Maiden scenario is an old story that gets told over and over. If archetypes were trees, you could liken that version to one of its leaves.

*

We went to see a movie once. We got our tickets and had some time before it started, so we went across the street to a mall to look around. We checked things out until it was time to head back, and as we were leaving, I accidentally bumped into this cute black girl in a purple sweater. She was going in as we were coming out.

After the movie was over, we came out, and walking across the street, we passed the same girl in the purple sweater, who was sitting at a bus stop. As we walked to the van, I said, "That girl was shopping the whole time we were watching that movie."

"I wonder what that means."

"What *what* means?"

"We saw her before the movie, and then again after."

"That's just a coincidence," I said.

"No. It's some kind of sign pertaining to our relationship. It's a syncronicity of some sort," she said.

"Oh yeah?"

"Yeah. You know what syncronicity is, right?" I'd read a little about it—it's the Jungian term for a coincidence that appears to be a bit *more* than coincidence.

"Wait a minute," I said, "you think us running into that girl, and then seeing her again after the movie is more than a coincidence?"

"Yes." She shrugged and took her keys out. We drove along for a little while. "You know," she said, "some people don't believe in coincidence. They don't believe there's such a thing as coincidence, that everything has meaning."

"Don't they call people like that delusional?"

"You're right, there is that type. Someone who builds connections between events, someone who relies too heavily on intuition—makes believe that thoughts are fact—and that's unhealthy of course," she said. "But the opposite end of the spectrum is just as unhealthy too. There's so much in life that's dismissed. There's so much color painted gray because people are caught up in the *myth* of science."

"The *myth* of science?"

"Yes. The idea that empirical science is the only way to know things is a myth. Scientists have become the new bishops. If you question the supremacy of science, you're in for trouble."

We drove on for a bit.

"And the girl in the purple sweater?" she said.

"Yeah?"

"It was symbolic for her too—it meant something in her life that she bumped into us, only to see us later."

"What did it mean?"

"I don't know."

"Why does it matter?"

"Maybe it doesn't."

"Then why mention it?"

"Because it might matter somewhere down the road. It just means, man lives in psyche."

"Man lives in psyche?"

"Man lives in psyche. It's a quote of Jung's."

"What's that mean?"

"It means this is all a dream. We're all living a collective dream."

*

That summer I was smoking and drinking as much as most people do in their twenties. I was never wasted around her, but there was a blip on the radar in the back of my mind telling me I was getting out of control. I told myself I'd put it together soon. And then we were lying around one afternoon, and she was on to me. She knew I was getting sloppy.

"How much pot do you smoke?" she asked very casually out

of the blue. I wasn't about to tell her, I figured I'd take it as a sign and tone it down from there.

"Not much, why?"

"I don't know, I was just curious."

"Do you ever smoke pot?" I asked.

"No."

"Why not?"

"I did when I was your age. Then once, I did it and felt stupid. Actually, I was in a kitchen with friends. We all had the munchies, and I thought about how we did the same thing the last weekend, and the weekend before. And I was suddenly repulsed to find myself doing it again. I was embarrassed."

"Oh."

"Do you drink much?" she asked.

"How much would you consider *much*?"

"Do you get drunk more than twice a week?"

"Sometimes. You don't drink, do you?" I asked.

"I'll have a glass of wine every now and then. Want to see something?"

"Yeah. What?"

"Hold on." She got up, went to her dresser, shuffled through some things in a drawer, and pulled out a picture. She brought it over, and sat next to me without showing it. Apparently she hadn't seen it in a while. She studied it.

"Let me see."

"I was your age," she said as she handed it over. It was her, nineteen or twenty, at a party, looking totally hot, and visibly buzzed. She was smiling. It was the smile of a really hot girl who knew she was hot and knew she had the attention of any man within view.

"See that face?" she asked.

"Yeah."

"That's a face of youthful hubris."

"What's that?"

"A trap you can fall into when you're young," she said. "It's the choices you make while drunk with youth that end up being so critical."

"Whaddaya mean?"

"You know how sometimes when you're drunk, the next day you wake up and wish you hadn't done something?"

"Yeah."

"Well, the same thing can happen while you're drunk with youth. You can do things then that unfold in a way that when you're older, you wished you hadn't."

"Got an example?"

"Well, this picture for instance," she said, taking it back and looking at it. "I was drunk at this party. A week or so after it was taken I had sex with my best friend's boyfriend."

"You did?"

"Yeah, I did. And when she found out, she never spoke to me again. And she was a great friend."

"Hmm."

"But, the same way you can make a bad choice drunk at a party, you can with your whole life, drunk with youth. You have to realize life goes on, and if you play around too long, a day will come where you're not young anymore, and the only thing you have to show is years of getting high and drinking beer."

"Hmm."

"It's just something to watch out for."

*

That October there was a fire in Malibu. The day it started they closed the roads, and I got stranded at her place. We were in her room messing around and reading poetry—she loved it read out loud—when we started smelling smoke.

We went out on the porch, and saw smoke coming over the ridge from Malibu Canyon. It got thicker as we stood there. The sun turned pinkish-orange. "I hope no one's house is in the way," she said.

"That's a lot of smoke," I said. I looked up at it for a minute then looked at her, and there she was, standing there, her eyes closed and her lips moving. She was praying. I'd never seen her do it and was a little shocked the way you'd be if you looked over at someone and suddenly realized they were praying.

"Are you praying?" I asked. She stopped and looked over.

"Yes. Do you want to?"

"Well, I mean...." I hadn't done it in years. I got kind of shy.

"You don't have to call it praying," she said. "Just consider it hoping for the best."

I stood there, *prude* about praying. "It's all right," she said, and kept praying as I looked back up at the smoke.

It was a pretty gnarly fire. It went on for a week. They closed down PCH from Topanga to Zuma. There was a swell that hit right then too—perfect surf—totally uncrowded.

*

I remember Halloween that year, she wanted to spend it together alone. We bought a couple pumpkins on a corner in the valley and went back to her place. We set out newspaper on the kitchen table and went about carving them up, her dogs and cats buzzing around. It's nice carving a pumpkin on Halloween afternoon, while some little black cat sniffing around keeps getting in the way.

She was a really good artist. She carved Pegasus, a flying horse, into hers. I carved a scary face in mine—tradition.

After we finished, we put candles in them and set them on the porch. The last bit of the sun dropped into the ocean as she cleaned up and I played around with the dogs and cats in the yard.

She had this big, old corduroy chair on the porch that looked out over the canyon and the horizon. It was green once, but from being outside it had faded to a golden-green. I got in it, then she came and settled in it too. We entwined a bit, and came to rest in a position where the weight is distributed just right and you're both comfortable and close.

The sun threw out a sunset, and we watched the animals play around. When it was almost dark she got up and lit the candles in the pumpkins, settled back in with me, and the animals settled down around us. We had a kiss here and there as the stars came out. We didn't talk a whole bunch, almost not at all. We just watched the light flicker in the pumpkins and listened to the wind in the trees and the leaves roll across the ground.

From the other side of the canyon, where there was a pocket of houses, we heard kids trick-or-treating. "You hear that?" she asked.

"Those kids?"

"Yeah."

3

Before I met Goddess Lady, whenever someone mentioned something about the unconscious, I always wondered what they meant. In order to explain it, I have to tell you the story about how I ended up in the hospital.

What happened was, my dad had just got his pharmacy—a pharmacist down the road was retiring—and one weekend they were going through inventory. I turned out to be the one transferring boxes from one place to the other, the temptation was there, and to keep a short story short, I got my hands on a bunch of pills. Mostly downers. I got pretty out of control with them. It all ended the afternoon my sister found me passed out in the hall. The next day I woke up in a private hospital.

The reason I tell you is because while I was there, I had therapy sessions with a doctor and he kept saying, "Your unconscious," or "In your unconscious," or "Unconsciously." Finally I was like, "Wait a minute—wait a minute—what *is* the unconscious? How does it work—what *is* it?" He made an analogy.

"If I turned off the lights in the room here, and it was completely dark, and we turned on a flashlight, what the beam of light lit up—think of that as your conscious mind."

"OK."

"If it was pointed at the phone, you'd be conscious of the phone, pointed at the lamp, you're conscious of the lamp. But even though the phone or lamp was lit up, there would still be other elements in the dark—the books, the pictures on the wall. If your mind were a room, and your consciousness a spot of light, there're still other things in the dark—in your unconscious."

That was the first explanation that gave me a way to think about the unconscious. Then hanging out with Goddess Lady, she got me familiar with other ideas about it.

I remember we were lying there once, and I asked her about Jung's quote, *The gods have become diseases.* "What does he mean by that?"

"I think he's talking about how Zeus, and Hera, and all the others, how their stories become manifest in the newspaper headlines today. Those myths, those stories with archetypal players, still surface through us. The gods were competitive, they lusted after one another and mortals, got jealous, started wars, murdered, had falls from grace—all the things that happened between gods back *then* are all the things still happening between humans *now*."

Then she told me she had read something and asked if I had ever heard of the Sumerians.

"They created the first civilization? The oldest, in Mesopotamia? The cradle of civilization, right?"

"Yeah," she said. "I was thinking, if they're the oldest known civilization—I got really curious what their myths were. I've just skimmed through one book so far, but it appears some of the Greek myths are originally told by the Sumerians."

"That's interesting."

47

"Yeah. And, ya know what's really interesting? They even have a story about the flood, and how one of their gods instructs one of the Sumerians to build an ark."

"Really?"

"Yeah. According to the Bible, the Sumerians are some old pagan culture, right? But the story of Noah, and the parallels with the Greek myths—together—isn't that weird? I think that's weird."

After hanging out with Goddess Lady and talking about heavy stuff, I'd end up at a party later, and try and talk about it, and no one would really care. They wanted to talk about who was doing it with who, or who had a lot of dough, the hot car—stuff like that. I wanted to talk about that too, but I also wanted to talk about heavy stuff.

I remember one night at a party down in Brentwood or Beverly Hills, some hip place, I was talking to this older girl in her mid-twenties. We were standing there, drunk in the midst of a swirl of people, when I started talking.

"I mean, think of it," I said. "If all these folktales from around the world have reoccurring motifs, and they're still showing up in modern-day movies, and they still hold our attention...."

"Oh boy," she said, and shut me up with a quick kiss on the lips. "Honey, you're too young to be this serious."

I had to wonder why I was all fired up to talk about things like that at a party. I guess it was all the books and ideas Goddess Lady was turning me on to.

When people would ask what I was doing, like at parties or hanging down at the beach, I'd say I was going to school. But I was just daydreaming and running wild. When you're in college you're either doing the work to get the grades to go on, or you're daydreaming. Everything at that point—besides hanging out with

Goddess Lady—was just *haste* to and for adventure—escape. I'd surf, then go make a trail through a canyon, or climb a peak. I swear, it was like I couldn't breathe unless I was paddling for a wave or making my way through some unexplored part of the mountains.

That summer was the real beginning of it all, when I really started to change. I started doing more stuff alone—especially hiking. Of all of the guys in our crew growing up, I think I may have always been the most keen on exploring and hiking. Sometimes it seems like you always see more animals when you hike by yourself. But that's one of the best parts about being in the wilderness—encountering animals. In the Santa Monicas, you see deer and coyote pretty often, way more than you see a fox or bobcat. Seeing a mountain lion is really rare. I'm pretty sure I saw one crossing the road one night, but I've never had a clear sighting of one.

There's something about spotting an animal that in a way is like winning a prize. I mean for instance, you're at the beach, and someone goes, "Oh look! A whale!" Everyone looks, and people go, "Where—where?!" and then, "Oh—I see it—right there!" and they're all excited. If they don't see it, "Oh it's gone now," the person who missed it is a little bummed. If the quote, "Man lives in psyche," is saying anything, and life is a dream, apparently it's a big deal to see animals in the dream.

Whatever it is about spotting animals, it's a good conversation starter sometimes—asking someone what the last animal they saw in the wild was. Or what their best animal encounter ever was. It doesn't always work—some people just go blank if you ask them that kind of stuff—but you have to love someone who'd take a minute to recount the most memorable animal sighting they had.

It was always a big deal for me as a kid to spot birds of prey—

hawks, owls, kites, kestrels. There aren't many eagles or falcons in the Santa Monicas, so to see one is a *really* big deal. I've seen eagles a few times, and a falcon once.

This one time I saw a bobcat though—which also illustrates what a daydreamer I used to be—is the most significant animal encounter I've ever had.

I went out to the San Bernardino Mountains one weekend with a friend. His girlfriend was a counselor at a camp, and with her girlfriend counselor, we were all going to have a double date. We drove up late, crashed out in the car, and early the next morning I got up and went for a hike. I started daydreaming I was going to find a suitcase full of money and I started to imagine how I'd spend it, how I'd go into small towns on my travels and give a grand or two to each community. I was thinking about that, hiking on a slope with pine trees, the ground a carpet of needles, when a spot came up that couldn't have looked more like someone had been digging and buried something. The needle carpet was all disrupted and looked like someone had tried to put it back and make it look natural. So what do I do? I find a stick and start digging. The soil was all loosened up—just like someone had buried something. I dug for about twenty minutes, then I got bored, gave up, and just sat down and took things in.

The stand of pine was sparse enough that dapples of light hit in places, and morning breezes were still going, creating that sound through pine—a sound you don't get in the Santa Monicas. I think John Muir once wrote about how when he was feeling lonely, roaming the California wilderness by himself, that the sound of wind through a stand of pines was like having someone there.

I was sitting there listening, watching the light change as the sun got higher, when all of a sudden this *huge* bobcat came walking up. He saw *me* before I saw *him*, and after he saw that I saw him, he *stopped* and *sat* about ten yards away. We checked each other out for a few minutes. I acted like he did, looked at him, and then blinked and slowly looked away. Then he got up and left. He didn't run or scamper, he just walked away without looking back. I remember the sound of the breeze as I watched him sway, paw to paw in that slender cat way, through the pines. It was unreal. That was my most memorable animal encounter ever.

*

Besides hanging out with Goddess Lady and reading a bunch of Jungian stuff, near the end of that summer things started to fall apart. I was doing crummy at the junior college, got speeding tickets, and lost my license for a year. I was drinking beer and smoking pot like a madman—just totally screwing up.

When I first started getting stoned it was pretty typical. Someone found their brother's stash, brought it to school, and afterwards we all snuck down to the creek and tried it out. We'd laugh, say stupid things—"I'll bet horses were so stoked when man invented the car!"—all the normal stuff when you first start getting stoned—and surfing and hiking stoned was always the best. But gradually, so I couldn't even see it happening, I started to change. I started to become introverted. I didn't care as much about what was going on socially—which is pretty much the opposite of how I'd always been.

At about that time I came across a book called *Steppenwolf*, by Herman Hesse. It's about a guy named Harry who's almost fifty, who goes around renting rooms in houses. He rents a room for a while, then packs up to rent a room somewhere else. He moves around because he's sold himself on the idea that he's got a wolf-like nature, and it blocks him from becoming part of normal middle-class life. In a way, Harry is like an older version of Holden Caulfield, who's finally had enough of all the phoniness of the world, and instead of accepting it, he opts to become a Wolf of the Steppes and exist on the fringes. I started to think that that's what was happening to me with all the running-wild stuff, that there was this wolf-like nature starting to develop in me. I could accept people wanted to hang out and talk about whatever the latest in cool was, but I wanted to escape it as much as possible. And when I did have to deal with it, it was the worst. If you're at a coffee place for instance, and the atmosphere's all relaxed and some guy comes in all nervous, talking in a halting voice with a broken cadence—no one wants to deal with that. Everyone else around will get all self-conscious too, and shrink away. If you're healthy, you naturally shrink away from something unhealthy. There's nothing wrong with self-consciousness sometimes, because everyone is at one time or another, but if it's because you're always getting stoned, making everyone around you uncomfortable, that's lame. And what's even more lame, I could've put a stop to it, I could've put a lance right through the dragon's heart of the whole thing. All I had to do was quit smoking pot.

There's a line in *Steppenwolf* that I've always remembered, "Man is the bridge between spirit and nature."

*

My landlady Grace and I had developed a relationship. We got along well. She started to take an interest in my life and made things easy, but she saw me starting to get out of control.

"What are you doing?" she asked one day. "You're wasting your time with school, you never go. You're driving around on a suspended license. You're always running off somewhere. You just seem so unfocused, and I'm worried."

"I don't know what's goin' on either," I said. My friends Jim and Matt had just moved over to Maui about a month before.

"Jim called and said you have a job over on Maui if you want it," she said. "Maybe you need a change of environment, maybe it'll give you a better sense of what you want to do with your life."

Grace offered to pay for the ticket over, and I didn't think twice about it. I wasn't looking at it the way I should've, that this cool lady who cared was offering a chance to figure stuff out. When you're passive like that, it's like you don't understand that you're not going to be twenty forever. A one-way ticket to Maui was only thoughts of surfing and hiking, and tourist girls.

I told Goddess Lady. "Why are you going?" she asked.

"I don't know. I really want to see what it's like to live over there."

"So this is like a vacation?"

"I don't know. Probably."

*

I got to the airport with a backpack and my board. I got on the plane and it was almost empty. I asked if I could put up the armrests in the middle section to sleep. Up and just off the coast, I watched Malibu pull further away. Then California was gone and I crashed out. Next thing I knew a stewardess was tapping my foot. I looked out the window and there was Maui. The tropical air swallowed me as I climbed off the plane.

4

I got my board and backpack, and went out to the curb. I hadn't told anyone what day I was going to get there, just that I was going to get there. At that moment I didn't feel too great. I was thinking about how there wasn't anyone around for miles— Pacific Ocean miles—I could really rely on. Yeah, I had a couple friends there, but really I was on my own for the first time. If anything happened, like if I broke my arm or something, I'd have to deal with it myself.

I hitchhiked over to Lahaina and found Jim. Jim is over six feet tall and solid. He has round features and a full head of black hair he always kept cut real short. He was probably the most talented of our crew. Not the best surfer, but the most talented. He could draw really well. Anyone can draw, like a hand or something, but to be able to make it come to life on the page, that's the talent Jim had. And he was in a band too, the bassist, and their group used to play parties. He was a stud. He was a good mimic, could make up little tunes, but he could get real serious too, and real quick. I'd seen him get in fights with bigger guys, and he never lost any I saw. He always used to start them with a phrase like, "Oh, you don't wanna do that…" or "Oh, you shouldn't say things like that…" or "Oh, you shouldn't act like that…" The next thing you knew, the other guy was down. I remember once where he was black and blue for a week.

We were all stoked to see each other.

"*Dude*, I can't believe you're here!" he said, "The surf's small today, but when there's swell, the harbor out front fires! The best little barrels!"

We dropped stuff off at his place and went for a surf. The Hawaiian Islands are so amazing. Out in the water, I looked around—over to the island of Lanai where the sun had just set, back at the West Maui Mountains glowing a tropical green, areas of earthen red near the peaks, then up at the clouds starting to catch fire with color. I started to get blown away about stuff like how big the world is, how far away the Santa Monicas were, how lucky I was, how scared I was, and how fantastic it is in those rare moments you're completely conscious of being alive. Sitting there in the clear, warm water of Hawaii, far from home, an intense sunset coming on, *I was alive*. It's weird to experience joy and fear at the same time.

*

I got the job through Jim and he let me crash on his couch for about a month before he had to boot me. I was so lame. It is tougher for a guy to realize he's a man than it is for a girl to realize she's a woman. A girl gets her first period and *bam*, she's a woman. A guy becomes a man as soon as he quits being passive, which can happen at twelve, twenty, thirty—sometimes never.

But it finally got to the point where Jim had enough. He got tired of dealing with my moodiness all the time—which was another aspect of the Steppenwolf stuff. If I was around people I didn't know, I was self-conscious, but around old friends I was moody as hell—especially in the morning. Jim had his share of fun with it, though. Skating to work, he'd ask questions, make up little songs. He even called me Moody for awhile. "Moody? Moody! Are you all right?! You seem a little quiet this morning. Say Moody, when you grow up—whaddaya wanna be?"

It got old and one day skating down Lahainaluna, he goes, "So, have you found a place?"

I didn't say anything. He stopped skating and told me to hold it.

"Look," he said, "I'm *serious*, you gotta find a place."

"I know."

"Whaddaya doin' then? You're not saving any money."

"How do you know?"

"Whaddaya think? We work together and you're sleepin' on my couch."

"I know."

"I mean, you're barely yourself anymore, Jack," he said. "You're always brooding, you barely smile. You're gonna get yourself in trouble if you don't snap out of it. You walk around in a daze. You're always reading that Jung book and think you're a philosopher or something—and you might be—but if you're not careful, things could get ugly."

"Whaddaya mean?"

"I mean, pretty soon here, I'm gonna have to say you can't crash on the couch—and then what're you gonna do? Sleep on the beach?"

"No."

"I've heard how it happens. Guys get over here and lose it."

"All right—all right," I said.

He gave me some more time, I made a couple half-assed attempts to find a place, and then one day he said, "Dude, I'm sorry, I got a date tonight, you gotta find another place."

Besides drowning in social situations, I was starting to drown in real life.

The first couple nights it wasn't comfortable, I barely slept at all. It gets a little cooler than you think down at the beach. The next couple nights I went up to Kaanapali where the resorts are, and snuck around parking lots looking for open cars to crash out in. Jim was cool enough to let me keep excess stuff at his place, so it wasn't like I was lugging a suitcase around Lahaina. I had a backpack with a change of clothes and stuff for the morning. I had a notebook and kept a journal. I definitely started writing poetry more. I have to tell you that too. It comes into play near the end of everything I have to tell, but I might as well tell you now. I write poetry. The first poems I wrote, I'd written as a kid. My brother found them in my desk drawer and mentioned it to the rest of the family on the way to the beach once. He didn't mention it in a mean way, but I remember it happening, and I was a little shy about it. I couldn't have been more than ten. I remember my first poem was about red being the color of the heart and blood, and how everyone's heart pumped blood, and everyone's blood is red, and that somehow that meant love was red too.

*

I hung out at the park by the Lahaina harbor quite a bit. There's a little park with palms in front of a small library. I used to go there and sit and read on this one wall. Some locals hung out there and I made friends with one. His name was Daniel. A full Hawaiian, he must have been close to forty. He was husky, with a broad face and big dark eyes—his mustache was like a Chinaman's, with long, wispy whiskers. He'd lived in Lahaina his whole life. He sold pot to tourists and usually had a beat-up guitar with him. After work, or if I was wandering around and he was there, I'd hang out, share a joint and take turns on the guitar. He played about as good as I did, just knowing a few chords, but he was always playing major chords, happy stuff, while I was always playing minor chords.

"Ho, brahda, you music always so sad," he said. "Play someting happy brah, play someting *happy*." He played left-handed.

"Hey," I said, "you play left-handed—just like Hendrix!"

"Shit yeah brah, Jimmy teach me." I smiled a *yeah right* smile. "No ree-ly, Jimmy visit Lahaina one year."

"Really?"

"Yeah, Jimmy sit unda da tree right on over dare—he play guitar and smoke *da kine all day long* brahda." I looked over at the tree near the corner of the grass closest to the water.

"You were just a kid then, huh?"

"Yeah," he said, strumming the guitar. "I was little den, used to dive fo da tourist quarters in da harbor all weekends."

Most locals were pretty aloof to *haoles*, but Daniel was cool to me. He'd even sell a joint if that's all I had enough for, didn't make me buy a whole bag.

Once after we got stoned, I was sitting against the wall staring across to Lanai, when he came over.

"Ho, wa you tinking bow brahda?" He sat down and I told him something about Jung.

"You always reading da books huh? I no like brahda," he said, "dey giving me headache, dey make da head hurt."

He didn't like to think about heavy stuff. I read something in *Paradise Lost* once. *Paradise Lost* is this long poem about the fall of the angels, and how Lucifer ends up becoming Satan, and what he does in the Garden of Eden. One of the lines in it is, "Know to know no more." When I read it I remembered Daniel saying books made his head hurt. Some people like Daniel know to know no more, I guess.

✳

Then one day I saw Matt out in the water. I'd known Matt since grade school. A white guy with freckles, average size, he was losing his hair a bit. He had a curly patch above strong blue eyes. He was one of the guys to start surfing first and was always one of the best. He could hit it so hard, just come square rocketing off the flats and up into the lip. He was always a man's man. Growing up he never fell in with the common tomfoolery. If a group of us were screwing around and talking shit and things went south, he'd usually be the guy to go, "Shut the fuck up, idiot." And he was usually right. He was high-man a lot too—the guy with the most cash counting out at the end of a parade. All the guys looked up to him—always confident, always seemed to know what he wanted, where he was going. He wasn't too smooth with the girls though. He'd get pretty nervous. He'd pull me aside at a party for advice sometimes, or I'd lead when it was him and me onto a couple girls.

He paddled out.

"Dude, where you been?"

"Hangin' out."

"I saw Jim, he said he had to boot you from his place."

"No, I—"

"You're not sleepin' on the beach are you?"

"No—"

"Dude, I won't be able to associate. I've seen guys punched out for that shit."

"I'm not staying on the beach." I lied and told him I'd met an older lady and was staying with her. He asked if I was working.

"Yeah. Same place."

"You haven't looked for a better job? That's the *primer* job. That's the one you land until you find a real job."

"I know, I'm just—"

"Go apply at Moose's, you can get on bussing and if you're cool and they like you, you'll snag a shift waiting breakfast."

I went in, applied, and got the job. They hired me on the spot because they'd just let someone go that morning. It was a restaurant on Front Street, the main street in Lahaina where all the tourists walk around. I told the manager I'd work as many hours as he could find. I was doing breakfast and dinner shifts a lot, only bussing though. I worked my ass off. I really wanted to save up and rent a room.

About a week later I ended up moving in with Matt and his roommate Marco, to split the rent three ways. Matt wanted me to because he was barely there. He had a windsurfer girlfriend from France who he stayed with a lot over in Hookipa.

Marco was an Italian-American and was pretty much everything I wasn't at that point. He had his feet on the ground, responsible. Short and balding, he had a big nose, big ears, and wore Dad glasses, the kind with no discernible style, just two plain, oblong lenses. He grew up in Massachusetts, had a degree in business and had done some traveling. The first night I moved in we sat around and drank beer. I asked how he'd decided on Maui. He had a raspy voice, talked from the back of his mouth.

"It was kind of funny," he said, "not like me at all—spur of the moment. I was working at a bar in North Carolina, reading the paper, listening to the news, and had been thinking about going somewhere else."

"Why were you thinking about going somewhere else?"

"I'd moved there for a girl," he said. "We were together in high school but it didn't work out—"

"Why didn't it work out?"

"That's a little personal, isn't it?"

"Sorry," I said, "I have a bad habit. I'm just interested in that kind of stuff."

"The reason it didn't work out? Sadly enough, I caught her with someone else."

"You actually caught 'em?"

"Not in the act or anything, they were making out though. Her lipstick was all over."

"Just caught red-handed?"

"She looked at me like, '*Oh well*,' like she was glad the truth was out."

"Then what happened?"

"I just went and got trashed, and moved out the next day."

"Whoa."

"Took me over a year till I ate and slept normally."

"Whaddaya mean?" I asked.

"Whaddaya mean, what do I mean?"

"You couldn't eat or sleep for a year because you broke up with a girl?"

"Yeah. Does that sound strange to you?"

"I don't know, maybe I've just never met a girl like that."

"Yeah, I was looking through an article about jobs on the islands. Then, later that day a couple came in, I got to talking with them, and it turns out they'd just gotten back from Maui—"

"Oh, so it was kind of syncronistic?"

"You read Jung?"

"Yeah," I said, "I mean, for the last few months or so."

"I don't know, Jung's a little far-out. Personally, I think Adler had it right. It's all about *Power*. Everyone wants it. It's all about making a minus into a plus."

"I haven't read Adler," I said. "I know he was another one in Freud's circle."

"Yeah, Freud is the one of the three who's discussed most—because he's talking about sex. Adler's talking about power, and Jung's talking about spirituality. They're all great, but I think Adler nails it. Everyone wants power—in fact, I think the drive for power overrides the drive for sex because the more power you have, the more sex you get."

"Depends on the quality of sex then? Power may mean more sex, but not necessarily the best kind of sex."

"Yeah, well the best kind of sex is subjective."

"What do you mean?"

"Some guys think a thousand-dollar-a-night hooker is the best sex. Some guys think their wife is the best sex. It's subjective."

"Oh."

"So what're you doing now? What're your plans?"

"I don't know, I'm…I don't know."

"You're still young," he said. "What're you—eighteen, nineteen?"

"Twenty."

"Yeah, you're still young. You got time."

"I don't know," I said. "Maybe I'm kind of a bum."

"You're a bum? Why would you say that?"

"I don't know, that's kind of the way I feel." I wanted him to tell me I wasn't a bum.

"You're not a bum. You're just young."

"Yeah—"

"I'll tell you what," he said, "I don't know you that well—not at all really. It was Matt's idea to have you move in. He wants to save some money. I make enough money, I don't need to split any rent, and I don't wanna lose this place, so I am taking a risk having you here." Because we hadn't told the landlord I moved in. "But I'll tell you what," he said again. "If you *are* a bum and I find out? I'll kick your bum ass out." The way he said it wasn't really offensive either—and he could've been too—he was one of those stocky, round-shouldered guys.

"Look, as long as a guy has a job, pays his share of the electric, water—buys his own food—you ain't a bum. My grandfather always said a boy becomes a man the moment he pulls his own weight."

Then he started to get a little buzzed.

"Why would you consider yourself a bum anyway? Because you don't own a car? A house? See, that's the thing with a lot of people," he said. "I spent some time in Europe and over there it's perfectly *fine* to be a carpenter or a waiter your whole life. It's perfectly respectable. Americans think that if you're not a VP or own your own business, able to say you're in land investment or the Internet or something, it's like you haven't really made it.

"Once you pull your own weight you're a man among men and it doesn't matter what your job is. Just pull your own weight.

"If you live in a society where the sky's the limit and you're not high up on the pay scale, there must be something wrong with you—right? That's the way the morons of the world have been conditioned to think."

*

A few days after moving in with those guys I was wandering around a bookstore when I met this lady. I was checking which books they had by Jung when she came into the aisle and started looking in the same section.

"Planning on reading some Jung?" she asked.

"Yeah, taking a look at what titles they have. Have you read him?"

"Oh yeah. Have you heard of Marie-Louise von Franz?"

"No—who's she?"

"Oh, she's incredible. So much easier than reading Jung. She was an analyst from his circle. I was looking to see if they had a book of hers, *Shadow and Evil in Fairytales*. I wanted to get it for a friend."

"I didn't see it." We looked. It wasn't there.

"Guess I'll have to order it."

"My name's Jack. What's yours?"

"Sylvie."

She was older, in her forties, and had gray-green eyes with a warm look. Although she had plenty of wrinkles, her skin was smoother than average. She was pleasant-looking. Her hair was dyed an orangish-brown that didn't completely hide the gray. It was bunched up behind, curly locks falling about. We decided to get some coffee.

"So, are you in college?" she asked.

"I started, I may go back. Right now—you know—waiting tables, surfing."

"You've got time—you *should* be waiting tables and surfing. And reading about interesting ideas—good for you."

"I don't know, I'm going through this weird phase. I've always been an extrovert—I used to be a class clown," I said. "But now I get all self-conscious, it's weird. It's like there's this wolf that comes out and makes everything uncomfortable."

She didn't say anything, just sat there listening, twisting the silver rings she had around on her fingers.

"I thought I could just go on forever, being me," I said. "But now it just seems like any charm I had, it's gone, and I'm turning into a freak."

"Well, it's never a bad thing to change. Change is growth. Unless you're growing in an unhealthy way. Are you using drugs?"

"I smoke a little pot."

"That could be part of the problem. But I suspect it's something more."

"Yeah?"

"Sometimes the Self has other plans," she said. "From what you describe, that you feel uncomfortable in situations you never had before, it sounds like a neurosis of some sort is developing."

"Is that it? I'm becoming neurotic?"

"From my understanding, there're times neurosis will occur in a person's life so that it isolates them. And even though it's painful to the person experiencing it, it's also protecting some new growth deeper inside. Neurosis can act as a psychic insulation sometimes."

"Whoa."

"If there is some sort of new growth going on with you, psychic change can be painful, so don't be afraid. Eat right, stay away from drugs, and you'll be fine."

She looked at her watch. I asked if she wanted to meet up again.

"Lahaina's a small town, we'll see each other." The flash in her eyes coupled with her smile was sweet.

I realized I hadn't been Steppenwolfish with her at all. And it was like that too, some people I'd totally start freaking out and others I wouldn't.

So I started thinking the whole Steppenwolf thing was a neurosis, and it was happening because there was something growing inside that needed some room to grow.

65

Then I went to see if Daniel was down at the park. There was definitely a voice inside that said, Don't—don't get stoned—be strong! But I was weak. He was there, we smoked a joint, and then, while playing guitar, he stops. All his attention is focused across the park. I look over, and there's a fight starting to take place. Three against two, and all of them were huge. Even though Daniel was Hawaiian and pretty big, he was actually small compared to some Hawaiian guys. These guys were all way over six feet—four feet across shoulder to shoulder, beefy—just huge. And they fought, and it was gnarly.

Tourists were running, screaming, moms and kids were crying. It took a few minutes for the three to overcome the two and even after they were down, they still kept on, kicking in the face and all. Don't ever buy into the idea that big guys are slower than little guys.

We walked over after it was over. Two cops were taking reports. Daniel went to where one of the guys went down and got kicked in the face.

"Ho brahda—check it out."

I went over, and there, in an abstract design of blood and saliva on a square foot of cement, was a tooth. A guy lost his tooth. All stoned, looking at it, I got this notion that if I kept smoking pot and screwing around, my life, metaphorically, would go from a nice conversation with a cool lady, to serious violence, resulting in a loss that can't be regained. Once you lose your tooth, your tooth is gone. With my toe I pushed it into a nearby crack. I remember every time I passed that spot, I'd look to see if the tooth was still there, and it was. Some guy's tooth that he didn't have anymore.

*

At the new job there was this really hot waitress. Her name was Jasmine. She was older, like twenty-eight, and really cool. I remember I was bussing her area, and I was clearing a table and asked a lady if she was finished with her breakfast. It came out bad, my voice broke—*screech*—self-consciousness. It made the lady and everyone at the table self-conscious and uncomfortable. My voice had been breaking all over the place that morning. I was back at the bussing station, staring at a plate of smeared yolk, breadcrumbs, and a parsley snip, all upset about being self-conscious, when Jasmine came up.

"Are you all right?" She'd been hearing my voice crack all morning.

"Yeah. I'm fine," I said. I felt like balling my head off to her— I think I'm losing my mind! I'm self-conscious! I'm turning neurotic!

She winked, gave my back a little rub, and went back out on the floor. She was a local, part Hawaiian, and had a stately bearing. The look in her eye, the cadence of her voice—she had a strong mind—a matriarch in the making. Some women you just know they'll be holding PTA meetings at their house one day, they'll be a force in their neighborhood. She was tall, and had light, looping-curly, brown hair down past her shoulders. Her eyes were light-brown and almond-shaped. Her face was angular and had fine cheekbones, a fine nose, and lips that were full and very kissable. A very sexy lady. Her teeth were incredibly sexy too. Teeth aren't the first thing you think of when you think of sexiness, until you come across a really great set. Straight and full— if you kissed her you'd practically want to lick them—her teeth were that beautiful. She smiled a lot too, so you got to see them pretty often. She was just special. You say everyone is special in their own way, but there's just no denying that some people are more special than others. Not that it's good or bad—it just is. She was one of those people who are just special, special.

At the end of that shift, she came over to pay out tips.

"Listen," she said, "I have to run some errands and things, but I'll be around later. Would you like to meet up for a bit?"

"Sure."

"Over in front of the library?"

"What time?"

"Three?"

"I'll see you there."

I got there early, daydreaming like mad about kissing her and going back to her place.

She came riding up on her bike.

"Hi." She rolled up and stopped.

"Hey there. How are ya?"

"Good."

"You want to go get something to drink?"

"Maybe another time?" she said. "I just wanted to talk for a bit, is that all right?"

"OK."

She put her bike down and we sat on the grass and looked out over to Lanai. The sun was still high, the ocean shimmered.

"I'm not sure what you're going through, but I know you have something to offer."

"You can tell I'm going through something?"

"Yes, you're young, you're growing. I understand the early years are difficult," she said. "Have you gone to college?"

"Almost two year's worth. I might go back."

"Well," she said, "I wanted to let you know things will be all right. You haven't found what it is you want, and that's a difficult place. Are you doing drugs?"

"Beer and pot—nothing serious."

"How much beer and pot?"

"Pot every day, beer on the weekends."

"Well, you might not want to do that."

"I shouldn't every day."

"I don't want to tell you what you should or shouldn't do. I just wanted to tell you I think you're neat, you say interesting things. I really get the feeling you have something to offer, Jack. I wanted to make sure you knew that. That's all."

We talked about the restaurant for a bit, then she said she had to go. When we stood up she asked for a hug. We hugged, I wasn't going anywhere with her. Then she gave me a peck on the cheek and got on her bike.

"You take care of yourself. The next few years might be hard," she said, "but just hang in there." She started to ride away, and then, looking back, standing balanced on the pedals, she said, "And try to eat more *whole foods* too!"

I don't know if she quit working at the restaurant or what, but I never saw her again.

*

Then I had my first, really weird coincidence with an actress I was crazy about. She was my muse at the time. I was into her right before I met Goddess Lady. I remember holding Goddess Lady up to her sometimes, wondering if Goddess Lady was too old for me and I should really be with the actress, who was hot and about a year younger.

I had bought some paper and watercolors and was doing a little art, and I needed some music, so I went down to the store and got some by a favorite old punk group. On the way back I stopped for a soda and saw a magazine with the actress on the cover. It had an interview with her in it, so I got that too. I get back, crank the CD, and do some art. Then later, I decided to read the interview, and it mentions how her parents took her to a concert of the same group I just listened to all afternoon. I didn't know what to think. I started to feel like I was in possession of some secret knowledge about how the world worked. Or that the world was aware of me. Or that some group of people was aware of me. Or that maybe even the actress was aware of me.

A few nights later I had this dream with her in it. It was so vivid, the kind of dream that stays with you through the whole next day. It was like we were just meeting, and I was my old self, and we were having a great conversation, and it was leading somewhere.

I was thinking about her a lot. I'd never met her and knew she had no idea who I was, but it was like there was this heightened sense I was about to meet her any second. That she was there on the island. That she was quite possibly going to come into the restaurant. It was like I was possessed or something, enchanted somehow, like I'd fallen into the abyss. My journal from then is just a bunch of entries about how I'd quit smoking pot for a few days, telling myself to keep going, followed by an entry about how I'd broken down, got stoned, and had to start all over. And a lot of notes about synchronicities. Like having a total in the super-market be nineteen dollars even, and then a few hours later overhear someone say it was their nineteenth birthday, and then later see a license plate that says nineteen—that kind of stuff. I wondered if I might've been on the verge of turning into one of those guys you see on the street, all dirty, giggling to themselves. It was scary. I just hung on to that idea that *all I knew* was that *I didn't know*.

Right around then, another waitress from the restaurant came riding up on a bike. I was going to do laundry and she saw me and came riding over. She was my age, from Mississippi. Blonde, green-eyed, she was really cute. She was really nice too, always smiling. She rolled alongside and asked questions, stuff like where I grew up. Even though things were soupy, something else was going on too. With her, it was the first time I made the choice not to do something because a girl might get hurt. She had blonde eyebrows and fair skin, so I knew what she had. And I'd want it if I could have it, but I knew if we started kissing, after it was over, I wouldn't really care if she was around unless I was horny again. I thought it through and didn't do it. Even though I might have been on the verge of becoming crazy, I was changing. I started to think about the girl before thinking about what I wanted.

*

There was this local girl. She was easy to relate to, she was one of the few people I was comfortable with at the time. She worked at a juice bar near the apartment. She was such a little fox. She was going to be a huge babe when she got older. Her dad was a white guy and her mom full Hawaiian, so she was a light-colored Hawaiian. Her name was Malia.

"Does your name have a meaning?" I asked.

"It means wind on the water," she said. "There're about a hundred words for wind on the water in Hawaiian—just like the Eskimos have a hundred words for snow."

She had hazel eyes, super-fine skin—tiny-pored, smooth and unblemished—smooth tiny-haired eyebrows, and light brown hair parted in the middle. Her hair was straight and super-fine, down to her ears. Of all the problems I was having dealing with people, I was always OK when I was around her.

I'd usually stop and get a smoothie on the way to work. She had smoothies wired. She was a crack-up, she thought she was such a punker. She always had some punk group on her headset.

She told me about her parents and how they wouldn't let her spike her hair or wear dark make-up, and how she'd have to sneak out at night, climb out her window, pillows under the covers, the whole bit.

One night after work I went over to the park, found Daniel, got stoned, played guitar awhile, then wandered over to Front Street. I was standing at the wall watching tourists window-shop across the street when I spotted her and her friends going along in a group. A couple of them had spiked hair, she had hers all slicked back. She was wearing a white T-shirt, Scottish-plaid punker skirt, and black army boots. I was watching her when one of her friends saw me, said something, and they turned my way. I looked away real quick. I'd never been stoned in front of her. I walked on for a second, then heard her call my name. I turned to see her running across the street.

"Hey!" she said, running up.

"Whaddaya doin'?" I said. "Did ya have to climb out your window?"

"No, I'm staying at a friend's. Her mom's cool."

"All right, so you're stoked!" I said.

She had a bunch of eyeliner and earrings that were little silver coiled snakes. She was such a little babe.

"What're *you* doing?" she asked.

"I don't know, just walk—" Right then she realized I was stoned.

"*Are you stoned?*"

"No—yeah. I mean—"

"You're *stoned!*" I was ripped. Her mouth opened in surprise. "I can't be*lieve you're* stoned. After all the times I've listened to you telling me pot is no good—you're stoned."

"I don't know, I was just playing guitar in the park, someone passed one around—I didn't want to be rude. *Geez.*" She shook her head with a smirk.

"Well, we're all supposed to be having fun," she said. "Even if some of us shouldn't be getting stoned—because they end up walking around alone on a Friday night!"

"I'm not walking alone, I just felt like watching tourists while I had my eyes open for packs of foxy girls."

"Listen stoner, I came over here to say *hi* and to tell you I want a kiss."

"You want a kiss? I'm too old—"

"I *know* you're too old for me. Don't look, but I have a bet with a friend over there, and I need you to give me a kiss."

"A kiss?" I started to look down the street.

"Don't *look*," she said, "You'll ruin it. Would you just *please* kiss me?" I looked at her and I kissed her. Like a two-second kiss.

"*Tha*nk you," she said. "That was nice. But I'm still mad at you for being stoned. You're grounded from smoothies for a week!" She flashed a smile, turned and ran back to her friends. For a while afterwards all the troubles of the world were gone. It's amazing, the energy of a girl.

5

Remember I said I used to steal? That I used to be a major klepto?

The first thing I ever stole was a box of crayons—not the one with sixty-four colors and the sharpener on the back—just a mid-sized one with like, thirty colors. I was six years old. I loved coloring that much that the thought of a new box of crayons with extra colors drove me to steal.

Of all the stealing I did, I never got fully busted—put in the back of the car, taken down to the station, the whole bit. I came close twice, both those times were at the Market Basket in Malibu. It used to be the Market Basket, now it's a bank and restaurant.

The first time I'd just finished a surf and a couple buddies and I were getting lunch. The routine was to surf all morning, go to Market Basket, pocket lunch, and then buy like, a single Tiger's Milk bar. I walked out and all of a sudden a tall grocer guy told me to hold it as he clamped onto my arm. I relaxed like I was going to go quietly, but as he led me back into the store, when the doors swung open, I jerked my arm away, bolted into the parking lot, ran under the bridge, and out into the field. It used to be a field, now it's a state park.

The other time I'd just stuffed a *Playboy* down the front of my pants, and as I was leaving, an undercover guy stopped me. Stocky, thinning hair—a guy like Marco—he would've chased after for sure. But what happened was, he poked his finger at my stomach expecting to feel a magazine, making sure he had a bust, but he poked an inch or two too high.

"Whadya do with the magazine?"

"I put it back."

"Good," he said. "I hope you learned something."

"It was dumb," I told him. "Sorry man."

I sat in my friend's truck, looking at that month's Playmate, realizing I could've been sitting in the back of a cop car on the way to jail. I didn't stop stealing overnight, but after that, the habit went on decline.

Out of the blue once, Goddess Lady asked, "Do you steal?"

"No," I told her. "I used to be a major klepto. I don't steal anymore."

"I have this theory," she said, "half of all *puers* are the type to steal, and the other half are adamantly opposed."

"Well I don't anymore."

"When you steal, you're only allowing a part of yourself to be stolen," she said. "Wouldn't it be cool if right after someone stole, a knuckle of their finger fell off, or their toe? So you could tell right away it wasn't something you'd do again?"

"Yeah."

"But! If they resisted the urge to steal the next time, whatever fell off would grow back."

"Yeah."

"Well, maybe they'd have to resist temptation like two or three times for it to grow back."

"Yeah."

Anyway, so I used to steal, and by the time I ended up on Maui I'd already quit for like a year. But then one night something happened. I was in a surf shop on Front Street, checking out boards. Cars were rolling past, tourists were shuffling back and forth. I was the only one in the store, the cashier was reading a magazine, and all of a sudden I started thinking that if I got the nerve I could walk out the door with a brand new board. They almost deserved it, they had the boards right next to the front door. It was that one thought though and before I knew it I'd picked the board I wanted and started checking the cashier with peripheral. I started rushing out, getting ready to steal, when the phone rang. The cashier turned around, and I did it. I lifted the board, stepped out the door, strode to the alley and out of sight.

Back at the apartment, I couldn't believe it. I stood there staring at a brand new board lying on my bed. It was such a rad board too. I was stoked, but I was bummed. I agonized about taking it back. If Matt or Marco saw it they'd know it was ripped off. It sat under my bed for a couple days until I came home from work and found them checking it out.

"*Dude*, where'd you get this?" Matt said.

"Whaddaya doin'?" I said. "Where'd you get that?"

"Under your bed—"

"Where'd ya get it," Marco asked. He was pissed. "I want it *outta* here—and you know what? You have a week to get your stuff out too."

"Marco—wait a minute—look," I said. "That's why it was under my bed, I was waiting for the chance to return it. I've been working. I haven't had a chance—"

"You gotta get some spray-paint to cover the logos," Matt said. He saw how rad of a board it was.

"That takes a lotta balls," Marco said. "It's fucked-up though. You could be in jail right now."

"I don't know what happened. One minute I'm standing there checking out boards and the next it was like—I swear, I haven't stolen anything for *a while*. I don't know what happened."

I kept apologizing but he wasn't convinced. I had gotten to know him pretty well—we liked to talk philosophy and stuff—he didn't really want to kick me out. He was hurt to find out I stole. That sucked. Matt helped smooth things out. He didn't want to give up the board, and he didn't want to suddenly start paying more rent.

"Dude," Matt said, "it's a stolen board—big deal. He realizes it was wrong."

"I don't want to see it again," Marco said and went to his room.

I took it up to Jim's. He was all stoked. The next day he took it to surf Hookipa and it got ripped off.

The whole thing got me thinking about fate and free will. It made me wonder what avenues in life would've become available with a different choice. Like if I would've never taken the board to begin with, maybe I would've somehow ended up meeting that actress. I mean, just as an idea.

The best analogy of the fate/free will issue for me though, is a balloon ride. You start out on the ground, your balloon ready to go. You could leave it at that and stay there your whole life, and there're people who'll live their whole life in the same town— nothing wrong with it. But you decide you want to go places. So you pull the cord that lifts the balloon and you're off. It took free will to pull the cord. Now a breeze sends you west—fate. You go along and then start to descend. Either you like where it appears you'll touch down, and do nothing, or you opt to pull the cord to send you high again—free will. There's definitely some navigation in life, but in the end you're lucky to land exactly where you wanted.

They say that fate is the result of inaction. Maybe it's that free will is your right foot and fate is your left foot, and you have to walk through life. No one goes through life hopping on one foot all the time.

*

I was sitting in the park passing a joint with Daniel and I told him about the board I ripped off.

"Ho brah, da karma happens pree-ty quick on da island. What goes comes back pree-ty quick brah."

What happened next, happened pretty quick. I got ripped off. Someone swiped my mask, snorkel, and money I had stashed under my mattress—coincidentally—the same amount the board I ripped off cost.

Because of that I had to ask the manager for an advance. He didn't like my type, he was pretty macho.

I'd been filling extra shifts, was never out sick, never late, and did a decent job. I went in early, asked for an advance, and the guy started hassling me for it. I wasn't in the mood. I told him I didn't deserve to be hassled about an advance by a guy who had no idea how to manage a restaurant. I got a check for everything owed on the spot. Sometimes getting fired feels great.

After getting the check cashed, and on the way over to find Daniel—see if there were any waves—I stopped to get a smoothie from Malia.

"Why don't you have a girlfriend?" she asked me.

"I don't know," I said. "I told you, I'm kind of in this self-conscious phase right now."

"I *know*, you told me, but I can't figure out what you're talking about. How come I never see it?"

"I don't know. It's partly because the day I met you I was having a good day and it never crept in from the beginning," I said. "If we discuss it enough though it'll probably happen, so let's change the subject."

"Well, I think you should get a girlfriend," she said. "And quit smoking pot! Maybe if you quit pot you wouldn't get self-conscious."

"I'd love to. It's not exactly that easy though. I've quit a hundred times. I mean I'm still quitting—I'm never gonna stop quitting."

"I'm bringing all this up because my sister has a crush on you."

"What? Your *sister*?"

"She's my half-sister, you've probably seen her. She works at the scuba rental place over by the park."

"The one with the long dark hair?"

"Yeah."

"She's your sister?"

"Half-sister." She was a babe!

"Her and her friends think you're cute. They see you walking around," she said. "She's seen you surf. But she said she's a little afraid because you're always, always—"

"Always what?"

"She used a certain word—I forget—she thinks you always look so serious."

"Did you tell her you knew me?"

"No."

"Why?"

"Didn't feel like it," she said. "I told her I knew who she was talking about though. I'm just saying this because I know you're nice, and I don't think you should be walking around brooding—that's the word she used—*brooding*. She said she's never seen you smile."

"What's her name?"

"Lori."

"I know what you're saying," I said. "Pot makes me brood."

"Well, why don't you take your *own advice* and quit messing with it?"

"Because taking your own advice is the hardest thing to do in life."

The diving rental place was on the way to the park. It was an open booth and as I was getting closer I felt my chest tighten up and my composure drop off to nothing, just totally self-conscious. I was thinking I could at least walk past with a smile, maybe stop and talk prices on a mask and snorkel. If I was the same guy I used to be, I would've got there in a flash, I would've practically run over to start up some conversation. As I got close, and she was there, she saw me and smiled. I looked away. It was *horrible*. If someone smiles at you and you don't smile back, it's the worst. I should've gotten my lame ass back over there, told her something for not smiling and asked her her name. In my mind then it was ruined though. Now she thought I was a creep. Which I was. I have to admit it. Just because I wouldn't quit pot. Just because I wasn't taking my own advice.

*

The next three days or so I smoked pot, read, and sat around the apartment thinking about how I'd lost my touch with girls.

80

I couldn't believe it—a total babe who was interested, a block away, and I had some neurosis because I wouldn't quit pot. Then, basically, I had a nervous breakdown.

It all came to a head one night, the night of my twenty-first birthday. I had to get someone to buy me beer because I'd lost my ID—that was the first thing. I mean, turning twenty-one, being able to buy your own, I couldn't even get that right.

I was going to drink some, and when Matt or Marco got home, go out and get trashed. But neither came home that night. I started to feel sorry for myself. Then I told myself to shut the hell up and that all the bullshit was my own fault because I wouldn't straighten up. Then it started raining. Then it started pouring. At least that cheered me up. I love storms.

So I'm sitting there, lights off, windows and front door open, wind howling through the apartment—I'd put pots and pans on my art stuff so it wouldn't blow around—when I start hearing this gnarly cat fight down below. I walk out to the railing and start listening to spits and snarls down in some bushes. Then it stops. It took my mind off stuff for a minute, and I'm standing there, drunk and getting rained on, when there starts this low, low-throated groan. It was the cat who'd lost the fight. It was sad. It was plaintive. And it got stronger and louder and cut through the storm. I imagined him not only losing the fight, but he lost the girl cat too. I'd never heard a cat groan like that. And it's going on and on, and I start thinking this is about more than losing the girl cat. Did he get an ear torn off? His eye scratched out? It kept going and going, the groan, and all this stuff started going through my mind. About syncronicity and how it was like I'd started looking for it, and how if you have an incredible coincidence go on, and then another, and another, it gets to be like a high. And it can get mesmerizing. And how I'd lost myself in the abyss of it all, and how I'd been in a battle with my unconscious and I'd lost, and was now going to slowly go insane. I just started bawling my head off.

After a while I calmed down a little, but I decided that that was it, something drastic needed to happen. I started thinking I had to go on a retreat out in the mountains. The next day I packed a lunch and headed to a spot in the West Maui Mountains to scout out a place to set up a camp. I was going to find a place and dry out for a while—a place to hike around, hang out, and hopefully get myself together. I'd seen one spot from the highway I'd been meaning to check out. It was a canyon that two major peaks rose up from.

Before the next day though, something else happened. I crashed out before Matt or Marco got home, and about three or four in the morning I got up to take a leak. I was falling back asleep, when from Matt's room I heard him saying my name. It's all dark, Marco's snoring, and I hear Matt go "Jack! Jack!" I get up, go to his door, just about to say What when he goes, "Dude don't! Don't! It's glass!" He was having a dream. "You're gonna cut yourself!" There was some silence, then he started mumbling. I turned to go back to bed, then heard, "I don't know dude, you're crazy. That's all I can say, you're crazy."

✳

I woke up, went on the hike, and found what I was looking for. Ten miles south of town, across the cane fields and into the canyon, was a canopy of trees next to a creek. I got back to the apartment and made a list of stuff I'd need. Sheet plastic, mosquito net, a cheap sleeping bag, a couple jars of peanut butter— that kind of list.

I told Marco.

"Jack's goin' native huh?"

"Whaddaya mean?" I said. "I'll get another job, I just need to get away for a while."

"Sounds to me like you're *running* away."

"Is it OK if I keep my suitcase here?"

"No," he said. "Look man, if you're running away—do it."

"I'm not running away."

"I've been keeping an eye on things and it's starting to appear that you are—in fact—a fuck-up. And I don't want any part of it. This is real life buddy. I don't know what you're thinking, but you're not eighteen anymore—you're twenty-one. Just because things get tough doesn't mean you drop everything and run away. Teenagers run away. So get your stuff and go!"

I bought what I swore would be my last bag of pot, hiked everything out there and set up camp. The plan was to get trashed for a few days, clean up for a week, and then go back to town.

I was tired and dirty and started feeling a little nervous and depressed. I looked at the camp I'd just set up and how pathetic it was. Then I saw myself for what I was. Just a little surfer fool who thought he'd charm his way through life, but now the harsh reality was setting in. I was pathetic, a guy full of promise, now standing dirty and alone next to a little plastic tee-pee and a backpack of canned goods. I started crying again. I kept thinking, Oh my *god*, what have I come to?

I start pacing around, whimpering, freaking, when I noticed a patch of mud that had happened from the storm the night before. It was a nice-sized patch of reddish mud, all smooth on top. Normally when you see a smooth patch of mud you might take a stick and make a design in it or something. But this was big enough to roll around in, and I was all dirty and freaking, and all of a sudden it seemed like the most natural thing to do was to lie down in it. And I did. I took off my trunks and sat down, wiggled my butt, and sunk in. It was all soft and warm. I can't tell you how good it felt. I don't know why, but it did. I buried myself in it, just got covered head to toe.

I rinsed off in the creek, dried off in the late afternoon sun, put on clean Levis, a clean shirt, and combed my hair back. It's funny what getting clean can do for you psychologically. If you're ever freaking on life, and there's a shower handy—take one.

The sun was getting ready to set. I ate some peanut butter and crackers and hiked to a view. I sat there and watched the sun set, trying to keep my mind off the situation.

The stars came out, and I was sitting there looking at them and started to review all the bad choices, all the blown opportunities, and was getting ready to beat the hell out of myself when a calm came over me. Out of nowhere, I was at peace. It was one of the weirdest things. It was an actual sensation. My chest wasn't all tight with anxiety, my thoughts weren't going a mile a second in distress, and I wasn't freaking about the future. Everything stopped. Everything was OK. I was at peace. It was weird. It was real.

I woke up the next morning and went for a hike. I was going to the top of the northern peaks. I stretched a little, drank some water, got stoned, and started climbing. I set off up a mound of lava rock that got narrower and narrower until it turned into a steep, slender ridge with a death fall on either side. It was like climbing a crumbling staircase. When I'd stop to take a breather, I'd lob a rock a few feet to my right or left and not hear anything for four or five seconds. Volcanic hiking is different, hiking up thin ridges, and on either side is the end.

I climbed for a few hours and got to the cloud line. The clouds hanging at the tops of the mountains were moving past, occasionally fusing out the sun. I sat down and took in the view—the coast, Lanai, Molokai—and did what you do when you get to a high spot like that—think about the world and daydream.

Running around the West Maui Mountains, I got pretty crazy sometimes. I'd rub mud all over myself, tear into mangos and star fruit, smear myself with the pulp. I don't know why, but I did that like once a day, or after a big hike. I'd rub mangos all over, roll around in the dirt and leaves, sit there and feel it for as long as I could, then dive into a pool and rinse off.

After a week or so I ran out of food and got bored. I hid everything to be hid and went back into Lahaina. I went up to the apartment and saw Marco. He was cool and said I could stay if I got a job real quick. I don't know why he did, but I'm glad he did.

*

I got another job bussing tables, and I was doing pretty good, wasn't smoking, then started to again. I remember smoking a joint with Matt. He was always stoned. It didn't affect him at all. He'd just kick back and blab away about whatever, with whoever. I'd used to be able to do it, but then I couldn't without getting all self-conscious.

"Man," I said, "you can still get high like we always used to."

"I don't know what your problem is," he said. "I mean c'mon, you're over here on Maui, you got a job, just hang. I don't know what you're doin' freaking out all the time. Just chill."

"It's weird. I just want to be like I always was—just surf and smoke and hang."

He mentioned a couple guys from San Diego over there

doing what we were doing—working and surfing. "Yeah, those guys kinda think you're a freak."

"Great," I said. "Do you think I'm a freak?"

"You're definitely not the same as you used to be."

"You mean you think I'm a freak?"

"No," he said. "But remember the other night at the park when we were all hanging, and then you got weird and said you had to go?"

"Yeah."

"After you left, that guy Rick was like, 'What's up with that guy?' I told 'em you used to be a stud, and that you used to scam all kinds of chicks."

"What did they say?"

"Nothing, just thought you were kind of a trip."

I couldn't quit smoking pot and I kept making all kinds of assumptions about things, just all spellbound and tripped-out. I was still staring into the abyss, and kept making people uncomfortable when I was around. I was bringing the whole party down. I didn't want to put anyone through it. I had to leave again.

6

So the new plan—or actually the latest version of the old plan—was to shine everything. To run away. Except this time, it was a suicide mission of sorts. Most suicides take place way before the actual act. Suicide is running away one too many times. There's this dictionary of mythology where you can look up all the gods and mortals associated with a particular subject. When I studied it, and counted the number of entries for each subject, *suicide* had the fourth most. Some philosophers believed that if you had a terminal illness, suicide wasn't a shameful thing. In *Steppenwolf*, Hesse says it's nobler and finer to be conquered by life than to fall by one's own hand. That rings truest to me—plus I've always had the notion that whoever does it—commits suicide—like if you're depressed and don't see things getting any better—that right after you do it and find out whatever you do when we die—you get shown what would've happened if you'd hung on and you go—Damn! If I would've just hung on! It's cliché, but you never know what tomorrow will bring. I've had whole weeks go by where all I wanted to do was kill myself—and then like a month later something happened, my life changed in a way that made everything bearable again. I got a new job or met a new girl or wrote a good poem or something. In the end, I can't argue around the notion that, unless you're terminally ill, it's nobler to be conquered by life than by your own hand.

You know, if you get bored or anything, just tell me. I'm happy to go on telling you all this, but just say so if I should stop, or you have other things to do.

*

Thinking I'd ruined my life and that I'd be nothing but a burden from there on out, I came up with the idea I'd paddle over to Molokai. One of the things that got me thinking about it was a bow and sling of arrows I'd seen in a garage. I passed it every day on the way to work. Then I happened to read an article on Molokai, and how it was less populated than Maui, had wilderness, and a bunch of wild pigs running around. I was good at archery as a kid, and I started thinking if I got hold of a bow and arrows, I could actually survive on my own until I found some kind of job and new life over there or something. I don't know what I was thinking. I probably couldn't have killed a pig anyway. I was out of my mind.

I ripped off the bow and arrows and traded my board for a big old one that would paddle faster. I bought a cooler and loaded it with stuff. Early in the morning I hitchhiked up to Honolua Bay, the best departure point. I got there and duct-taped the cooler. I had water in a backpack for the way over. I attached the cooler to the leash and set off. It was about eleven miles to Molokai. I thought about sharks, but was so depressed that if I was going to get eaten, fine.

So I got out into the channel and there's a swell. I remember I sat up on my board to get some water. I looked in both directions to either island. It was gnarly being out that far on just a board.

I stuck my head in the water and looked down, rays of sun shot straight and danced into the richest blue. As incredible as it was, looking into it gave the same type of feeling of not wanting to look behind you while walking alone in the dark. Out that far, you didn't want to see some huge creature swim into view.

Then came the wind. It picked up quick. The swells started to whitecap, breaking. It was a huge hassle. I kept paddling but pretty soon started to get blown away from Molokai and Maui both, towards Lanai. A little while longer and I started chafing on my shoulders from the backpack, and I started to freak about getting caught out there after sundown. I didn't care about sharks before paddling out, then I started caring. Then I got pissed at what an idiot I was to even be out there in the first place, and went back to not caring if I got eaten. My shoulders were going raw in a couple places so I had to get the backpack off. I looped the leash through it, which helped. I kept paddling, freaking on my bullshit, thinking and saying one thing one day, doing just about the opposite the next. Someone once said we're never more true to our nature than when we're full of shit—which makes knowing someone who's full of very little shit one of the great things in life.

Anyway, things aren't good, the wind's really going, it's getting late, and I see a boat. It's in my direction but going to cross my path a ways in front of me. Yelling wouldn't have done a thing. The only way I'd get picked up is if they saw me. My trunks were florescent green. I took them off, sat up on the board, and every time I got to the top of a swell, waved. I did that for a few minutes, when I saw someone come out to the rail and look in my direction. Luckily, within a minute they were on the way over. I put my trunks on and paddled my ass off, imagining shark fins right behind me.

It was a thirty-foot fishing boat, there was a Japanese/ Hawaiian guy at the railing.

"Hey, how's it goin'?" I yelled. He didn't say anything. The boat slowed about twenty yards away and an old man came out.

"What the hell you doin'?" the old guy said. He looked like a bald, tanned Santa Claus with sunglasses.

"Nothin'—I was just trying to paddle over to Molokai." He looked at me, said something to the Japanese/Hawaiian guy, and went back into the pilot house.

"We leavin' sheethead, betta get ya ass in da boat pretty quick!"

I paddled to the stern and climbed on board. I got everything on deck, the Japanese/Hawaiian guy whistled, the engines revved and we were off. He went into the pilot house. I stood there and looked at their catch. They had about a dozen dorado and a couple of massive tuna. Within a few minutes I was shivering. A few minutes more and I got the nerve to poke my head in the pilot house. The Japanese/Hawaiian guy was crashed out on a cushioned bench against the wall. The old man was sitting at the wheel. He turned, looked me up and down, and turned back.

"Thanks for picking me up," I said. He gave a nod. A whole minute or two passed before he said something.

"What was that you had strung up to your paddleboard?"

"My stuff."

"Where were you going?"

"Molokai."

"You were planning on staying on Molokai?"

"Yeah."

"In trouble with the law?"

"No. I just kind of needed to get away." He didn't reply. We fished twice more on the way to Lahaina.

Pulling in the harbor there was only a faint light on the horizon. I was not happy to be unloading a board, cooler, and bow and arrows in front of a bunch of tourists. I was hoping Daniel wasn't out in front of the library.

The Japanese/Hawaiian guy pulled a truck around to the landing. I helped unload the catch. The Japanese/Hawaiian guy said something like, "Get 'em job, punk," got back in the truck and left. The old guy took some money out of his pocket and handed it to me.

"This is for the work you did."

"I can't take money from you!"

"Look, I did you a favor, you did some work. It was worth it to me." I took the money.

"If I could give you one piece of advice?" he said, his brown eyes steady, serious.

"Yeah?"

"There's not a day that's going to arrive in your life when you wake up and from there on out everything's easy. So don't believe it's just around the corner. Whatever life you're given—rich, famous, or in love—it will never be easy. There's not a day that's going to come and from then on all your troubles will be finished. And the sooner you accept that and find what it is you do well—and get to work at it—then life gets easier. But it'll never be plain easy. It wasn't meant to be."

He wished me luck and got back on his boat. I got my stuff back to the apartment in two trips, I had to go back to get the cooler. I sat on the couch in the dark and winced over and over at being the biggest piece of shit in the world. The next day I returned the bow and arrows to the garage.

7

After that I was just sullen. Totally dejected, it seemed like it was just a matter of time before giving up and becoming a literal *bum*. Then I almost died.

It was a big day at Honoloua. I had that board I'd tried to paddle over to Molokai, so I could handle bigger surf. The wave faces as they peaked were in the fifteen or twenty-foot range. It was the biggest I had ever paddled out into. I took off on my first wave, rode it, kicked out and thought, Yeah — Big Waves — No Problem. A few dozen guys in the line-up, I paddled back out and sat up on my board, full of myself. Then all of a sudden, everyone's down and paddling. On the horizon were dark-blue lines of ocean — huge mountains, marching in. To see that is to understand how the universe, in its physicality, is totally indifferent to everyone. It doesn't matter who you are, if you don't get out of the way, you're over. That's the reason nature is so perfect, it doesn't play favorites — rich, poor, talented or not, athletic, disabled, beautiful, less than — we're all the same in the path of a ten-foot wave.

Everyone in the pack scratches past the first wave and I decide to take it. I flip my board around and paddle hard. In big waves, with so much water moving upwards, you have to really get your board pointed down the face and dig that last stroke before getting to your feet. Your instinct is to get to your feet as quick as possible, but you have to commit to that last dig even though you want to get up. I didn't, didn't have enough momentum, stood, and got pitched. In the air and on the way to the flats below, I remember seeing a guy paddling off the shoulder, looking up at me like, Dude you're *bummed*.

I hit and was carried full circuit with the arc of the wave into the violence of the white water. In waves that big your body is ricocheted around, on the verge of being torn or crushed. The force and power are incredible. I made it back to the surface just in time to see the second wave peaking up and pitching. To have a two-story building crashing towards you is pretty scary. I was in the impact zone. I took a deep breath and dove in fear. My leash went taut as the wave grabbed the board and sucked me back in. I popped up from that to see the third wave of the set pitching. I get as good a lung-full as I can and dive. Same thing, the wave grabs my board and I'm sucked back in. I pop up from that and there's another, even larger, peaking and pitching. The middle wave of a set is usually biggest. I dive again, panicked. I feel the leash pull, then go slack. It broke and the thought crosses my mind I might become a statistic. I pop up again to see a huge wall of white water. The foam on the surface is almost as thick as my head and I have to splash it away to get a breath. I didn't even get a chance to dive. As I'm getting worked, the calm, sunny cliffs above fill my mind. If only I was there. I need air. I start to fight for the surface, not sure which way is up. I need air, I need air, I need air, *right now*—and then it happened. My life flashed before my eyes. I swear, it's an actual phenomenon. Your whole life can flash before your eyes. Stuff of you riding a tricycle when you were four, kissing a girl by the lockers, learning to drive, taking pictures at someone's wedding—everything. That was the last thing I remember, my life flashing before my eyes. I came to coughing water. The only thing I can figure is that somehow I unconsciously fought to the surface. I should've drowned. If you paddle out and it's big, and you pick the first wave of a set, you better make sure you make the drop.

*

The next day I went for an evening surf at the harbor and got my face sliced open.

I was out in the water about an hour, the sun went down, and I was on a last wave in. It was a little close-out tube. I dove off my board, was in the white water, when all of a sudden—Bang. The tail of my board slammed into my face. One of the fins glanced off my cheekbone and gouged down into my cheek. I sat up on my board, touched my fingers to my face and felt a good-sized, jagged flap of flesh. In the twilight my fingers were covered with dark liquid. I paddle over to the docks. The tourist faces told the story. This one lady was like, "Oh my God! You need a doctor!" I went over to a little emergency center nearby. I knew of it because one night working, I'd cut my leg carrying a bag of trash out from behind the bar. The guy wasn't an expert at doing stitches, and when I got there, it was the same guy. My cheek was completely gouged. We both agreed I should get over to the hospital. The guy was cool and taped a patch to my face.

I hitchhiked over. I got to the front desk and told the nurses I didn't have insurance. They had me fill out general information, then told me to wait. I sat in the emergency room for a bit, when a guy walked in with a hot lady. They were all dressed up to go out, or they had just gone out. He was a plastic surgeon. He looked at my face, "So you don't have any insurance, huh?"

He gave the nurses some orders, took some pictures, and next thing I was laying on a table and he was sewing up my face. He was kind of showing off for his date. She was sitting right there watching and he was telling her about all the different muscles in the face, that kind of stuff. She was totally into it.

A couple weeks later I went back to have some of the stitches taken out. The guy was really pleased with the work. He took some more pictures and showed me off to other doctors down the hall. Before I left he said, "I did you a favor—next time you see someone needs one, you take care of it."

✻

You can get staph infection from surfing reef breaks in harbor water. A cut from coral on a wipe-out or paddling at low tide, and pretty soon your ankles and wrists start itching. You itch until the skin breaks and a scab forms. Then the next morning or getting home from work, the scabs, which still itch, have pockets of pus under them. Then you go buy some hydrogen peroxide. If it gets really bad, you have to get antibiotics. It started to get bad. I called Grace. "Come home!" she said. She missed me.

Next thing I was hitchhiking on the corner of Lahainaluna, headed back to Malibu Lake.

8

It was a sunset flight back home and the colors spread out over the ocean. If you're ever flying home over the ocean, try to get a sunset flight.

I was sitting next to a businessman and asked what he did. He'd just closed a deal for his communications company, said his wife would be waiting at the airport.

"What about yourself," he asked. "Where are you headed?"

"I followed some friends out to Maui to see how I'd like it," I said. "I guess living there wasn't for me."

"Well, it's not always easy to find your place in life," he said. "Sometimes you have to fight for it." He told me not to worry, and not to give up. He got really serious, tapped me on the forearm and looked me in the eye. "If there is any final judgment on a life, you don't want it to be said you gave up. There'll always be screw-ups, but never give up."

He went over paperwork and I stared out the window at the fading colors. I looked down on the blackening Pacific and wished I could jump into it, just slam into the cold vastness and perish without a trace. That's how I felt, like giving up.

*

I came across the word *nostalgia* once. The roots are the Greek *nostos*—homecoming, and *algos*—pain. Painful homecoming. Most dictionaries list it as a wistful yearning for something removed in time or space. If you look up *wistful*, you get *pensive*, which means dreamily thoughtful in a more or less sad way. And of course if you look up *dreamily*, you get dream-like. Driving along Malibu Lake on the way back from the airport, I stuck my head out the window and the smell of chaparral gave me a haunting pang of nostalgia. The scent of the Santa Monicas always gets me dreamily thoughtful. It's the sage and chaparral meeting the ocean air, or the scent of Santa Anas moving through oak and sycamore. That always does it to me. I've tried to figure it out. It's definitely a wistfulness, a pensiveness, but still there's another element to it too. It's like a longing coupled with a wonder. Nature can be so beautiful that it can strike a human with awe, and being struck that way brings about feelings of gratitude. It's like the longing is caused by the situation of never being able to truly bond with something you are grateful towards, that you love, but is totally indifferent to you. A scent in the air can strike that in me. A scent that gives way to a sense of the timelessness of nature, which gives way to a wistfulness about being mortal and a longing for immortality. Maybe. I guess. But that longing is always buoyed by the gratitude of experiencing nature's beauty. Sometimes you have to wonder if humans were made to marvel.

*

I called Goddess Lady and left a message that I was home. She called back and we met at the Reel Inn on PCH near Topanga. It was a little over a year since that day we met in the canyon. She came in late and looked awesome. She had on a tank top, those girl pants that go to just below the knees, and flat sandals. I didn't realize how much I missed her. We hugged and climbed into a seat. She took off her sunglasses and there were those amazing blue eyes again. Ruby-blue, emerald-blue, star-blue, I don't know what name blue, but they were always so amazing to see. All I wanted to do was eat her up. I wanted to be back at her place showing her how much I missed her, and how much I never realized just how rad she was.

"Any new boyfriends?"

"Yeah, we met a couple months ago. He's an arborist. We get along pretty good." It was all I could do to play it cool.

"You look awesome," I said.

"Thank you. So what do you have planned now that you're back?"

"Well, I think I'm having some kind of psychic something happening."

"What makes you think that?"

"I feel weird."

"How?"

"Like I'm spellbound. Every time I turn around it's like some rad syncronicity is going off."

"For instance, like what? What's an example?"

"There's this actress I like, and I bought a magazine that interviewed her, and the same day I bought a CD by an old favorite band. I get back to my place and in the interview the actress mentions the same band I'd just got a CD of."

"Hmm."

"It's just an example, there're others. I have a bunch written down in a journal. It's like I'm chasing down this mystery—what does it mean that I see an advertisement for German chocolate cake, decide to get a piece because I love it so much, and then later that night, some talk show host has a skit with German chocolate cake in it? What does it mean?"

"Well, you have to be careful."

"Careful about what?"

"You could be headed towards dangerous territory, or you could be going through a process that will one day help you make a valuable contribution—something great. But the unconscious is a powerful thing. It's the big inside."

"The big inside?"

"Nature—the physical universe—is the big *outside*, the psyche is the big *inside*. That's what Jung meant when he said, man lives in psyche. Somehow what's outside and what's inside are just two aspects of the same thing. If you walk into a jungle or forest or out into a desert, you couldn't just go along without being on guard, right? There're animals that could kill you, oceans and rivers you could be swept away by, the elements. Same thing with the big inside. You can't just go around, chasing down synchronicities without being on guard."

"Hmm."

"In his autobiography, Jung says there was a period where he studied himself and at some point realized he might lose touch with reality by following a never-ending trail back into the forests of the unconscious. Maybe you should read that right now."

"I will," I said.

"But you're still keeping your journal?"

"Yeah."

"Well, like I said, maybe you're going through the process every genuine artist or thinker does."

"What do you mean?"

"Where you're going through that Promethean thing. That thing of the artist or thinker who brings back art or ideas to revive whatever has become stagnant. That fire that creates hope. To do that necessitates a trial, a situation where you break away from the crowd and venture into realms of the collective. Some artists pull it off. Some give up because they sense the risk is too great. And some never make it back."

"You mean they go crazy."

"It's dangerous—yes. If that's what's going on with you right now Jack, then you need to know it's nothing new—you're not some sort of messiah who's going to save the world once and for all with whatever you find—but you need to be careful."

On the way out she gave me a hug and a kiss, and I got that sinking feeling when she got in her car to leave.

"They say it takes a long time to make an old friend," she said.

"You mean we're not old friends already?" I joked. "And here I was thinking we were old friends." She smiled.

"You know you can call me anytime, right?"

"Yeah."

"How about I'll call in a week or so?"

"OK."

"Oh," she said. "I read a book while you were away. It might be just the thing to read right now, along with Jung's autobiography. It's called *Shadow and Evil in Fairytales*."

"By Marie-Louise van Franz?"

"You've heard of her?!"

"Over on Maui."

*

After that, I went deeper into the abyss. I just had a rash of synchronicities, one after the other. I was just observing synchronicities, not really thinking one thing or another about them. Just kind of duly noting them. I remember this one. I was reading *Moby Dick* right then. Even though it's a huge book and seems daunting, it's really not that hard to read at all. I had just gotten to the part about scrimshaw, and then later that day ended up at a girl's house, and on her shelf was a whale tooth with a whaling scene carved on it. I was having stuff like that happen all the time.

Also, I was in a creative fit. I got painting supplies, and blinds drawn, music cranked, I painted. I painted and wrote poetry like a madman—just this intense desire to create—like I didn't have a choice about it. It was an actual phenomenon. I could write a poem about anything. If I needed a subject I'd flip through the dictionary, look for an interesting word that evoked something and build a poem out of it.

One night I was flipping through when I found *Eos*, the name of a goddess. The Goddess of the Dawn. She brings up the sun after its night-sea journey.

Deep and dark is the night when/ a glow growing brighter/ sets the skies ablaze./ Eos, oh so beautiful,/ Eos, such a sight.// Her rosy fingers stunning the clouds with color./ The morning waters celebrate her face/ once again before turning blue.

A couple nights later I had a dream. I was alone on a mountain somewhere in the Santa Monicas and it was dark. Then came the dawn. It started to get light. And when the sun broke the horizon, when the first rays burst into my eyes, set within them was a speck of something. It was a tiny silhouette way out on the horizon. Trying to figure out what it was, I suddenly realize it's approaching. Closer I see it's a woman, flying without effort. Tilted forward, her arms down along her body, one knee slightly raised to divide the sky as she rushed towards me. She was wearing some kind of robe and I could see it and her hair beating behind her as she approached. She arrived with a *whoosh*, and there she was, floating before me. She was a goddess—a real goddess. Her eyes were violet and looked right through me. I couldn't make out anything in them other than an indifference— the indifference that an immortal creature might have while gazing upon a mortal. I guess. I was drawn to her, but there was something foreboding—something deadly. I don't know what made me sense that, that she was deadly, but I did—the way you sense things in dreams.

9

The guy who ran the sales crew heard I was back from Maui and called.

I had started door-to-door sales when I was eighteen. We were skating a ramp at the end of a cul-de-sac and we noticed a guy knocking on the doors of some townhouses. Someone asked what he was doing and a few nights later we all had on gas station shirts, going door-to-door. It took a couple nights to get the hang of it. We'd sell these little plastic books with an oil change and radiator flush to homes and businesses within three miles of a certain station. They were a good deal if the station was honest. Sometimes you'd find out the station was a rip-off and you couldn't sell books for them—at least I couldn't.

There was a crew of us, fast-talking nineteen- and twenty-year-olds, making more than guys doing forty hours a week. We'd get to surf all day, go sell between five-thirty and eight-thirty weeknights, and party the rest of the time.

We'd meet up near the station we were promoting, drink coffee and drive waitresses berserk with crude stories told too loud.

You see a lot of stuff when you go door to door. There are screwed-up people, mean people, but for the most part everyone's cool in their own way, and you can tell, waking up in the morning, life's pretty much the same for everyone. Sales is determining intelligence and sensibility in the quickest amount of time and then adjusting your pitch accordingly. Body language tells a lot, eye contact and voice tell the rest. If you're selling the same thing long enough you know right where to go. And you can rely on little quips to make them laugh, all that. In the end, no matter how quick or long a sale is, it all comes down to one rebuttal. It's that one rebuttal that makes the sale. Period. Every time. It's got to be strong. In whatever sense. If it's not there, no sale.

I may have been stuck in the abyss, but I'd said the pitch so many times that I could still make sales. I lost more sales than I did before I went to Maui, but I could still make them.

Of course going door to door, you were always looking to get laid. It didn't happen that often, but it happened.

I walked up some steps of a house in an equestrian neighborhood and rang the bell. A few seconds into waiting and I heard a horse on the other side of the driveway. Around from the side of the house comes this huge black horse, a total babe on top. She was unbelievable sitting there in her black boots, tan chaps and red T-shirt. She was about thirty, fine raven hair parted in the middle down to her neck, green eyes like water, and rich red lips all full.

"Hi, how ya doing?" I asked.

"Can I help you?" Her voice was firm and even.

"My name's Jack, and we're doin' a promotion for the Chevron. The one in Malibu Canyon?"

"OK."

"I'm sure you drive your own car, right?"

"Yeah. But it's brand new. I take it to the dealer." Whenever anyone said that at the door, you had to have that solid rebuttal or the sale was over.

"It's under warranty?" I asked.

"Yeah."

"Great! All our mechanics are certified—and dealerships are expensive. They'll charge you seventy bucks just to rotate the tires. With our promotion you get the basic service that your dealership charges to validate your warranty—you get it with us for free."

"Oh really?"

"All the guys down there are state-certified, just like your dealership—you can cover your warranty—and if you like the way an oil change is done, you'll be familiar with a place close by. That's worth something by itself, knowing a mechanic down the street from your house. "

"Could you do me a favor?"

"Sure."

"Can you stop back in a few minutes?"

"Sure."

"I just went to my dealership, and it was expensive, so I do want to take a look."

"OK. I'll go talk to your neighbor. My name's Jack."

"OK, Jack." She started to turn her horse around. "If I don't answer the bell, come around back to the stable."

"OK."

I went and tried to make a sale. Sales build confidence. I got back to her place, rang the bell and hoped she didn't answer. I wanted to go around back to the stables. I did, and found her fluffing a flake of hay for her horse.

"What's your horse's name?"

"Pegger."

"He's rad."

"Thanks. He's my brother's."

"Where's yours?"

"Up north."

"What did you name yours?"

"I didn't name him, but his name is Dancer."

"Oh. Well, so you drive your own car, it's under warranty, and you take it to the dealer?"

"Yeah." I gave her the pitch, she was definitely going to save money.

"Can I see it?"

"Sure." I walked over and handed the book to her. Her eyes were so green and her nose made her look like a huntress goddess to me—forty-five degrees, sharp as opposed to turned-up like a sprite or nymph. Her skin had *adventure* about it. She had a heartiness a lot of goddesses don't have. She wasn't a porcelain skin–type goddess.

"Anyone in the family can use it anytime in the next twelve months," I said.

"Anyone in the family can use it?"

"Absolutely."

"OK, you sold me. I'll get one."

"Great."

"Let me get my checkbook."

"OK."

"Could you do me a favor?"

"Sure."

"Could you throw that saddle in the back of the jeep out front?"

"Sure."

"Thanks. I'll meet you out there," she said, and disappeared into the tack room.

I carried the saddle around front, threw it in the jeep, went up to the front door and sat down on the steps to fill out the book.

After a few minutes she walked out, looking into her checkbook.

"Who do I make this out to?" she asked. I told her the name of the advertising company.

"So you don't work there at the station?" she asked as she sat down next to me.

"No. I just go to the doors. I didn't say I worked there, did I?"

"No."

"Does it matter to you if I do or not?"

"No."

"Sometimes, for some sales, people really want to know you work at the station."

"Is your name really Jack?" She filled out the check.

"Yeah."

"So this is what you do, this is your job?"

"Yeah." She was so hot. I wanted her so bad.

"It must be difficult to face people telling you no."

"Nah, either they can save money or they can't."

"Are you going to school, Jack?"

"I was. I've been thinking about signing up for classes again."

"Do you have any idea what you want to do?" she asked, tearing out the check.

"I'm not sure." Her name was Claire. She had neat hand-writing. "I like your handwriting."

"Thank you."

"I just read this book about how you can actually change yourself by consciously changing your handwriting."

"That's interesting."

"Your handwriting doesn't really slant to the left or right— very straight up and down. I think that means an independent mind."

"Hmm. Graphology, right?"

"Yeah. If I ever hire someone for a job, or rent a place to someone, I'd have a brief questionnaire. You can find out a lot from someone's handwriting."

We talked, it got dark, and then I heard the horn. The routine was that the van would honk, and if you didn't jump out in the street, it meant you were making a sale.

"Is that your ride?" she asked.

"Yeah."

"What are you doing tonight?"

"Nothing. To tell you the truth, I'd love to just sit here and continue hanging out."

"How would you get back to where you came from?" The horn honked again going past the house.

"My car's not far away. I could get to it."

"Do you have ID on you?"

"Yeah." I took my driver's license out of my shirt pocket and handed it to her.

"Where's your wallet?"

"I don't have one."

"You don't have a wallet?"

"Just cash and an ID."

"Do you want something to drink?"

We went inside, and her house had a good smell. That's one of the things about doing door-to-door, you smell a lot of different houses. What's weird is, there are distinct smells. There're certain smells that are the same for more than one family. For instance, there's this one smell I call the Beagle smell. I call it that because when I was a kid there were some people we used to visit, and they had this smell to their house I really liked. They had two beagles too. Their house didn't smell like beagles, but every time we went there I always petted their beagles. Every now and then,

I'd knock on a door and there'd be the Beagle smell. There're about five or six different smells. There's the Asian smell. A lot of Asian family homes have a certain smell because of the type of food they eat, and they barely ever open their windows. There's the Indian smell—very curry—and they barely ever open their windows either. There's the Dingy smell—a lot of white and black people have that one—and them too—they barely ever opened a window.

You'd get bummed making a sale at some places where you had to go in while they filled out a check and you had to hold your breath for ten minutes. If it was really bad, sometimes I'd say I had the flu so I could stay outside. It always made me wonder how I'd be going along on some rad sunny afternoon, knocking on doors, and there'd be people hanging out in stuffy houses with the windows closed.

The smell in Claire's house was nice. It was a nice big place. I told her.

"It's my parent's—it's where I grew up."

We talked about art and poetry. We had some wine and somewhere in the middle of the second glass we collided. All alone and then bam, right there in the living room, just the most incredible sex ever. Her body was so unreal. We did it like four times. After one of the times, lying there, she asked me where I saw myself in ten years.

"I haven't really thought about it."

"You're twenty-one, right?"

"Yeah."

"Do you have any goals?"

"To be honest, I just want to read, and learn, and create. And I just want to do something good."

"Do you have any goals?"

"Not really."

"My dad always said, a soul without a goal is lost."

"What is a lost soul anyway?" I asked.

"If someone asked you, what would you say?"

"I've always thought of a lost soul as a ghost."

"Yeah—a ghost. A ghost of a person, because they never found a place to put roots down. I want to tell you something." She turned to me and propped her head on her hand.

"You're smart and you're handsome, and you remind me of someone I knew. You really need to focus on finding out what you want to do in life. You're twenty-one. Yes, there're late bloomers, but you just remind me of this guy I was with when I was your age. He was like you. Bright. He had a gift for gab like you. But he never focused any of his talent onto goals. Last I heard he was living in an apartment over in some run-down part of the valley. I just wanted to tell you that. I hope you make up some short-term and long-term goals and start doing whatever it takes to reach them."

We did it until the early morning and then she drove me to my car.

"So can I have your number?" I asked.

"I had a great time, but I have a lot of things going on in life right now—can I have your number?"

"Sure." I gave it to her.

"I'm down here occasionally. Maybe we'll meet up again."

"OK."

I took her advice and I wrote down some goals. One of them was to go back to school to get my associates degree. I signed up for the fall semester.

10

I had about twenty units to finish. I did school in the day and sales at night. Between classes I started to spend a lot of time in the reference section of the library. I began to get immense pleasure flipping through encyclopedias, dictionaries—anything with facts about reality—the whole man-lives-in-psyche thing. Theories about what comets really are, the entomology of scarabs, the atomic number of mercury, the origin of pi—stuff like that. I'd flip through and stop at anything that captured my attention. Like life was a dream and a visit to the reference section was dream interpretation.

*

Then it was late October again and the Santa Ana's were going. I came home from school, cleaned the corral and fed the horses. There was a good swell so I shined sales to surf glass-off. I had my board and suit in the truck and was looking around to make sure I had everything when I noticed something on the screen of the sliding door. It was a big green bug. There weren't a bunch of other bugs around or anything, there was just this big bright-green bug smack in the middle of the gray screen. It was a type of grasshopper. It had crimson eyes and wings that looked like leaves. It was pretty magnificent. I checked it out and then went for a surf.

I remember it was epic that day too. Zuma is a world-class wave when it's breaking. The barrels were way overhead on the sets. The swell direction was from New Zealand and the conditions were perfect. The sun near the horizon shot through the back of the waves. Flying through was weightlessness, zooming through a space of golden-emerald liquid. There really is such a thing as flight for a human on this planet. It's surfing. It's true.

As I drove home, the bug on the sliding door crossed my mind and I wondered if it'd still be there. I was really hoping it was, like a clue to a mystery that I could go look up in the reference section.

It was still there. I got a flashlight and checked it out. It was still there the next morning too, and driving to school, I was hot to find out what kind it was. I got to campus and went straight to the library.

Finding an encyclopedia of insects, one with color pictures, I flipped through and found it. It was a cicada.

I was on my way out of the aisle when my eye hit upon *Dictionary of Classical Mythology, Symbols, Attributes & Associations*. It's the same one I told you about before that lists gods and mortals and their stories. I checked the copyright and contents. I went a couple pages further in and one of the first entries was *abduction*, and right there on the list was Eos, Goddess of the Dawn. When I wrote that poem and had that dream, it never occurred to me she had a story other than that she was goddess of the dawn. Like that was all she had time to do. After the latest production of dawn, she had to start work on the next morning—right? The thought of her having her own story never occurred to me. I practically broke out in a fever to find out what her story was. I got three different books down because when you're talking Greek mythology there's always variation, and one book might have a different version of a myth or mention some obscure aspect you won't find somewhere else. Sitting there Indian-style on the floor of the aisle, I started to read about her.

Of all the goddesses, she was considered by all to be one of the most beautiful. She was so beautiful that another goddess got jealous—in one version it's Hera, in another it's Aphrodite. The most prevalent story is that Aries went after her, and out of jealousy, Aphrodite put a curse on Eos that she'd fall in love with mortal men. There was a list of guys she'd abducted—Clytus, Orion, Cephalus, Tithonous. I wrote it down and some other stuff and then it was time for class. Ironically, it was my *logic* class, which I happened to be trying to pass for the third time. Truth tables killed me.

I got to class and was all inspired to start a rough draft of a new poem about Eos. I started moving around some of the phrases I'd copied down as notes. The dawn evokes a mysteriousness./ Chromatics displayed as fragility/ personify an evanescence so incompatible/ with the carnal nature ascribed—/ who has she abducted now?

After that, I went into design mode. I would make designs in the margin of the notebook while listening to the lecture. Before I knew it, class was over and people all around were getting up to leave. Then I noticed something. While I had been making designs I had drawn a square around the first letter to one of the names on the list of guys she had abducted. I hadn't paid attention when I'd done it, just totally unconscious. All the other names remained as I originally wrote them except one— Tithonous. Who was *he*? What was *his* story?

The story is, Eos was flying along one morning, saw Tithonous and carried him off. She loved him so much she asked Zeus to give him *immortal life*, but forgot to ask for *eternal youth*. Zeus made him immortal, but didn't give what she forgot. They had some sons together, and as the years went on Tithonous started to age. Eos didn't. He grew older and older, and being immortal, never died. Then one day, not being able to stand seeing him so old and withered, she turns him into a cicada.

Did everyone have coincidence like this go on? Did everyone have it go on, but only crazy people pay attention to it? Was God trying to get my attention? Was nature trying to get my attention? Was Nature God? I didn't know. I just went into *all I know is that I don't know* mode. I *did* know I wrote a poem about Eos. I did know I had a cicada attached to the screen—which led to finding out more about Eos—which led back to the cicada. It was a pretty elaborate synchronicity, and it involved an unconscious aspect of myself, because I did not remember putting that square around the T.

11

It was right around then that I guess I'd gone on to the next level as far as discovering more about the unconscious. I remember I was at a friend's and a few of us were watching a movie. I happened to be sitting in a chair at one end of a couch. Three people were on it, someone else in a chair at the other end. I was seated so that in the glow and shadow the movie cast, my peripheral vision picked up something like a synchronization of arm and leg movements. Like two people would scratch an itch at the same time, or cross or uncross their legs together. After that I got into a phase where I studied body language going on between people hanging out. Just noticing stuff like when two people would take a sip of their drink at the same time, or which way two people standing in conversation had their toes pointed. You find there's a whole dialogue of body language going on when two or more people are gathered. Just as creatures do, we transmit our feelings through body language. For instance, if a girl's feeling indifferent, there's body language for it—if she's interested, there's body language. It's almost magnetic the way a body reacts to another body. And when it's happening, a person isn't really aware of it. It's not like anyone goes, OK, now I'm going to use this body language to display blaa, blaa, blaa—body language just happens.

If you study that stuff long enough, you start getting glimpses of an entity, a very elusive though definable entity, that reveals how a person's ego is only an aspect of the entire person. It's like a person's consciousness is a small circle floating within a larger one, and the larger circle is part personal but also spans to the collective level—the creature level. It's paradoxical. It's something that is always there, though rarely reveals itself. It reminded me of that saying that when two or more are gathered, God is present. Back in church, when they said God lives inside you, or that your body is a temple of God, I never understood it. But that's what checking out interaction between two humans made me think after a while, that there was this whole unconscious creature/god aspect to us.

The next semester started and I had an anthropology class titled Magic, Religion and Witchcraft.

12

The first day of class, I saw this hot death-rocker girl. Doll-like features, dressed in black, pale skin, black mascara, long hair dyed dark orange. She was like a Beautiful Halloween Girl. I didn't think anything would happen between us. I always tried to get the hot death-rocker girls in the past. The quiet mysterious thing going on that you wanted to get to the bottom of, but they usually weren't into sun-bleached, pink-nosed surfers.

On the second or third day of class she came in late and sat next to me.

The professor, this tall, lanky gray-haired guy in his sixties, was starting the lecture. That day he was talking about primitive man. He wrote a name on the board.

"Now," he said, "I can likely guarantee no one has ever heard of Lucien Levy-Bruhl. He's out-of-date these days."

I got Jung's autobiography, which I'd been reading, out of my backpack and flipped to the page to make sure it was the same guy.

"He studied primitive societies," the professor went on. "And to him the primitive mentality is *prelogical*—or mystical. To a primitive a thing can be itself, and at the same time, something entirely different. A forest can be a forest, or something else—a sacred realm where initiation takes place. A lion can be a lion, or something else—the incarnation of an ancestor, maybe. To the primitive, something can be A, and *not* A at the same time. Civilized peoples, affected by science, can't think like that. To us, a tree is a tree—not a tree and something else at the same time. In other words, the primitive mind can accept what civilized minds would consider contradictory. Levy-Bruhl came to the conclusion that both kinds of thought—the rational and the mystical—exist in every human mind, with one mode or the other in control at any single moment."

I got Beautiful Halloween Girl's attention, and pointed to Levy-Bruhl's name. She knew what I was getting at, about how the professor said no one in class had ever heard of him. She got wide-eyed and her mouth dropped open.

So we started messing around.

I was still doing the door-to-door sales and she kept asking if I wanted a job working for her dad. He was a special effects artist for the movies. I finally decided to take it and the next day I was on set waiting to be told what to do. It was a movie with a famous actor, about a guy getting hassled by aliens. In it there were two different types of aliens—those ones with the big black insect eyes, and these other little green ones. The green ones had costumes where the face had remote-controlled parts and it was my job to work the movements in the mask from off-screen. Making movies is capturing consciousness. A film can change consciousness. It's all screwed up these days—not being able to talk about the truth—and we get films that are more product than pieces of art. But still, even if it's a formulaic piece where you know the end before the thing is halfway finished, it's still capturing consciousness.

13

Beautiful Halloween Girl's dad used to sit in his office and read books all day. Every morning he'd show up with a cigarette and coffee in one hand, and books in the other. I always checked what he was reading. He read everything, but lots about politics and the government. Sometimes he'd sit in his office and read all day and not come out to start sculpting until late afternoon. He was a real artist. He had a couple scrapbooks of commissioned work he'd done over the years, like for city buildings and shopping centers. I remember pictures of a huge statue of a horse and rider commissioned by some whiskey maker back east.

He could go on for hours about the government and how everything was a bunch of lies and how we were all screwed. I was clueless about politics at that point. I always assumed we elected people to Congress and they did the best they could with what they had. I knew a little bit about conspiracy theories, but I'd never really gotten into that stuff either. I may have had weird coincidences go on in my life, but I've never seen a UFO or anything. I mean, I've never even seen a ghost. I've talked to people who say they have, but I never have.

I remember a discussion with Beautiful Halloween Girl's dad about the movie.

"What do you think of all that? All the alien conspiracy stuff," I asked.

"Sure you want to know what I think?"

"Of course."

"You could make the case that aliens are running the world," he said. "That they're tending to us like we tend to farm animals."

"No way."

"You ever hear the term, bread and circus?"

"*Bread and circus?*"

"It's a term Roman senators used to describe how they controlled Roman citizens. You give people comfort and entertainment and you can run around the outside and run the entire show. TV advertisements show us living a comfortable life but only twenty percent of Americans can afford that life. They're the *patricians*—their job is to keep the one or two percent who control everything in power. The *powers that be* have control of mass communications and popular information, and when you control that, you can get people to believe whatever you want them to— including that complete lies are the truth."

"Who are the *powers that be*?"

"The ruling class."

"The aliens?"

"No, the people keeping the whole charade in place—if we are in fact being controlled by aliens. I've never said I know one hundred percent for sure that we are. Maybe there are no aliens. Maybe all the problems are just because a bunch of slimy patricians and ruling elites are screwing everything over."

"Whaddaya mean, screwing everything over?"

"We could have free energy here in America, but don't, so a very few Americans can maintain their control of the energy industry—that sounds like getting screwed over to me. And that's only one example."

"Yeah."

"It all comes down to money and whoever's behind the curtain—alien or human or both—they have control of Congress, the first branch of government—the will of the people—the balance of power. The establishment WASPs are the ones doing their dirty work."

"Who are the establishment WASPs?"

"The people who stay out of the news. All the names that go way back in America that you never hear about. The people of New York City, Boston, Washington, D.C. All the people the impresarios party with."

"*Impresarios*? What's an impresario?"

"Impresarios are the people who say, 'Good evening, and here's the news....' They all know the same dance."

"What's the dance?"

"The dance is called divide and rule."

"*Divide and rule*?"

"You put up your Republican puppet, you put up your Democrat puppet, you get the impresario to ask a question about sex or violence or religion, and you use the show to influence public opinion. That's how the few have always controlled the many—with opinion."

"If we are in fact being controlled by aliens, or alien-like people," I said, "and we're getting screwed and we can't really tell because of all this bread and circus, and divide and rule—there's still got to be some way out of it—right?"

"I don't know if there is. I've been searching for the answer for decades. I haven't found it. Maybe you can."

"If I ever start looking for the answer, where's a good place to start?"

"The summer of 1947."

"What happened then?"

"Truman signed the National Security Act. It created the Pentagon, the NSA, CIA, and then later, NASA. Americans have been living under that cap of disinformation ever since."

"And you don't think anything can be done to bust it open?"

"Not as long as corporate interests control the information allowed over the airwaves."

*

The relationship with Beautiful Halloween Girl didn't work out. I remember she wanted me to get a tattoo but I wasn't into it. She was always going to the clubs down on Sunset, hanging out with all the rockers. I liked going down there every now and then, but not as much as she did.

Right then, this guy from the alien movie called. He was an electrician I got along with. His name was John. He was in his late thirties. He was one of those older guys who could still live like a kid, but acted like a man when a man was needed. All the hot make-up and wardrobe ladies got all excited when he walked by. He knew about Jung and archetypal stuff too. We had some good conversations. He asked if I wanted to work on his crew. They were going to be at airports a lot, and in the jet hangers, and he knew shots were going to call for work up high. He knew I liked heights because I always climbed up to where they were working when I didn't have anything better to do—so he called to see if I wanted the job.

On a movie set there are the camera crew, the electricians, and the grips. The camera crew does the cameras, the electricians set the lights, and the grips flag them so no light spills into the wrong part of the shot. There are other groups, but besides the talent, those are the three main ones you need to get a film made. The grips and the electricians are the ones who have to go high. "Send me high, or send me home." It used to be only guys did the job, now you see girls doing it too. On the big sound stages of the old studios, the perms are seventy feet up, a network of beams to walk along to hang lights and stuff. They're not forgiving. There's a long list of grips and electricians who've died making movies. Even though they have to be able to go high, most will avoid it if they can. I was always willing to go up so John and the older guys were stoked. The jet hangers were different than the perms are on sound stages too. Sometimes you had to walk along a steel truss with a death fall on either side.

The sound guy had seen us up there working. "Check this out," he said, and handed me a book.

"What's it about?"

"Check out the chapter, 'The Mohawks in High Steel.' I'll bet you get a kick out of it."

It was about New York City and some of the Native Americans who built the bridges and skyscrapers way back when.

"I don't know how you guys do it," he said. "I almost faint just watching." I told him thanks for turning me on to the book. I thought it must have been a cool syncronicity for him that he was reading it and saw us guys working on high steel.

On that same movie, at the airport all the time, we started doing all these shots with helicopters. There were usually two or three of them on the set each day, and one of the pilots was this beautiful, twenty-something girl. That was her job, to fly helicopters for the movies. She was really shy. One time I was talking to her and she mentioned she flew charters on the weekends.

"Look," I said, "you might think this is crazy, but there's something I've always wanted to do. I've always wanted to tie a rope inside a helicopter, wrap it around my arm real good, and stand out on the skid while being flown low and fast over the ocean."

"Whoa," she said. "That sounds awesome! I'll do that! It's pretty expensive to rent a Jet-Ranger."

"I'll see if I can get a couple guys from the crew interested. I'll tell them they can party in the back seat."

"OK!" She was totally into it.

We were going to meet at the Van Nuys airport Saturday morning and both the guys called all hung-over, saying they couldn't make it. That meant I had to pay for the whole thing myself, or no go. It was a lot of cash but I had to do it. I wanted to fly low and fast over the ocean. That's how I always imagined the gods doing it. Like when Hermes goes to Calypso's island with news for Odysseus.

I get there and there's no one in the office and there's no one around out front. I go sit on steps that look out over a bunch of different kinds of planes parked on the tarmac. I'm sitting there for about fifteen minutes when this old gray-haired guy pulls up in a brand new black Jaguar. He's kind of short and stocky, barrel-chested, and he goes to the trunk, pops it open, and starts pulling stuff out. There was no one else around so I decided to go over and take a look.

"Say, you happen to know anything about the charter company over in that trailer?"

"They fly charters around LA," he said.

"I was supposed to meet the pilot but no one's in the office."

"Probably out on a run." The stuff he was pulling out of his trunk looked like parachutes.

"What's that for?"

"In case my jet konks out."

"Your jet?"

The guy was a wealthy businessman who'd bought a 1965 Czechoslovakian fighter jet and outfitted it with brand-new everything, including a top-of-the-line jet engine. His buddy who was supposed to fly with him that day cancelled. I told him I had cash for jet fuel and before I knew it I had on the chute.

"If something happens," he said, "I'll pop the canopy, try to roll the plane upside down, and you'll fall out."

Right then the Helicopter Girl showed up. She saw me with the parachute on, I told her what happened, and she was totally stoked for me. "Tell me all about it at work!"

As the engine lit up and the black skid marks on the runway accelerated past, I was pressed swiftly back into the seat as we took off.

We went out over the desert. Off one wingtip were the mountains where I grew up and off the other was the Sierra Nevada range.

The jet must have been the old guy's exercise machine. He put it through its paces and that meant serious physical exertion. I'd read once that fighter pilots sometimes squeezed their legs and butt together as tight as they could because it helped keep blood up in the brain while pulling serious G's. I wondered if the old guy wanted to see if he could make me puke. We did a few turns where you were so scrunched into your seat little stars started forming at the top of your field of view, streaming into a loss of vision as the blood was pulled out of your head.

"How you doing back there?"

"Great!"

Once he saw I could handle it he started flying in a way that it feels good. He'd put the thing on its tail, get to the top of a loop, roll, and the earth and sky rotated around your weightless body.

*

Grace mentioned her nephew was having problems and that he might need a place to stay. He got caught for stealing something, from someone's house or something. He moved in the next week. We didn't get along very well.

I was looking forward to working on another movie with John, but at the wrap party he gave me some bad news.

"Jack, you're great. You did some really great work," he said. "This whole movie I've been trying to make up my mind whether to work another or take a break. I think I've decided I need a break."

"Oh—that's cool."

"I've been meaning to travel for a few years now. I got a ticket to India. I'm going to land there and wander back home."

"Like just go wherever you feel like going, as long as it's closer to California?"

"Yep."

"Maybe you're like Harry Haller in *Steppenwolf*," I said.

"You read that book?"

"Yeah, didn't I tell you? I tell everyone about that book."

"I read it too," he said. "Sometimes I wonder if I'm some kind of Steppenwolf. I really would like to find a woman to share with though."

"Maybe you will on your way home."

"I'm going to be forty. That's what I'm hoping."

Before he left, John gave me some numbers to call for work.

*

This is right about the time I told you about in the very beginning where my friends were all on my nerves, and my screenplay got sent back, and living with Grace and her nephew was getting awkward.

Then my dad in Santa Barbara called and said he could use some help up at the pharmacy and I ended up moving into the Castle.

14

So I was working for my dad's pharmacy and on a sunny spring day I'd just bought some juice and was on my way out of a 7-Eleven when the cover of the local weekly caught my eye. There was a picture of a girl on it. She was hot. Her name was Edie Sedgwick.

Edie Sedgwick was a girl from an establishment WASP family whose members have played various bit parts in American history. A great-great-great-grandfather was friends with George Washington and Alexander Hamilton. His daughter wrote a novel that was well-known at the time and she gave teas where writers like Hawthorne and Melville would attend. A grand-uncle was an editor of the *Atlantic Monthly*. Her father and brothers all went to Harvard.

Her father was the first to move out west. They had a place in Goleta for a bit, then moved over the mountains to the Santa Ynez Valley. Then sometime in the 50s, they found oil on their ranch. Edie took her inheritance to New York where she hooked up with Andy Warhol and all these characters who inhabited a Manhattan studio known as The Factory. She was in movies, modeled for all the fashion magazines, was *Vogue* Girl of 1965. She was hot, hip, rich, her black Rolls limo seen in front of all the happening places. Throughout the article were excerpts from a 1982 biography about her.

After getting some meds to a convalescent home, I stopped off at the downtown library to see if they had the book. They did. It had pictures showing a whole slice of Americana I was unaware of. Pictures of twenty-somethings dancing, posing, and hanging in 60s New York—making art, little films and stuff. I checked it out and then got a call from my dad to pick up a prescription at Cottage Hospital. I had never made a delivery there but had to go back twice that day. Later that night I start reading the biography and it mentioned how Edie was born that very same day, at that very same hospital.

The next day I was taking a break between deliveries and I pulled off into the Earl Warren Showgrounds to read. I had parked there before because it's centrally located and if my dad paged, I'd be able to get wherever, quick. So I'm sitting there, reading along, and it says how Edie's dad was a sculptor and how he sculpted a horse and rider and I turn the page and there's a picture of the very statue I was parked in front of. The hairs on the back of my neck stood up. All I knew is that I *didn't* know. Sometimes it seemed like I was living more of a dream than reality. Sometimes it was like a high and sometimes I didn't like it. Sometimes I felt like I was being hunted. I didn't know what was happening exactly but I knew something was. I remember getting on my hands and knees a few times around then and praying that whatever was going on that I did something good with it. I may have been prude about praying in the past but I sure wasn't at that point. Whatever it was, it wasn't over either.

A day or two later I went to go pick up a lady named Valerie. She was a customer of my dad's and I delivered meds to her once a week or so. She was born and raised in Santa Barbara. Back in the 60s she was coming home from her classes at the community college, walked in on some guy robbing her apartment, got raped and almost killed. Her skull was fractured but she survived. She'd gone through years of therapy, and when I met her she was this cool lady recluse. She was tall and skinny. She had a large face, big eyes, and thinnish lips. She looked like that famous billionairess Doris Duke. She wore her graying-black hair slicked straight back to where it was chopped a few inches below her ears. She wore black wraparound sunglasses and chain-smoked filterless cigarettes. She was on a few different meds so her motor skills were off. Her hands were always shaky. She'd seem all there most of the time, but other times, in her own world. Occasionally I'd take her places when she needed a ride. I remember I was picking her up to take her to her psychiatrist. A *People* magazine started flapping around in the back.

"Do you mind if I hold that magazine?" she asked. "That flapping is going to drive me insane."

"Is there something back there to throw over it?"

She reached back, got it, and took a look. "Are you reading this magazine?" she asked.

"Someone left it in the pharmacy," I said. "I was reading the article on Prince Charles."

"I find it bothersome how much nonsense is peddled these days."

"Whaddaya mean?"

"There're three types of people. Those interested in other people, those interested in events, and those interested in *ideas*. This tabloid mentality—lurid affairs, so people can gloat—it's repellent. There're no ideas in this."

"I agree there's a fascination with dirty laundry, but there are ideas in those magazines too."

"Do you have an example?"

"Well, the article on the Prince of Wales mentions how he's been hanging out with Laurens van der Post, who was a friend of Jung's. You know Jung?"

"Oh yes," she said. "I read him for quite a while."

"Well, as you may or may not remember, he's got this quote, man lives in psyche. If man lives in psyche," I said, "and if life is one big collective dream, it's interesting the Prince was pondering things from that perspective."

"And you find this interesting?"

"Yeah."

"And this idea that life is a collective dream, are you trying to interpret the dream by sifting through information found in tabloids?"

"For what an article indicates about our collective experience—yeah—maybe there's something like an interpretation. If it's insightful."

"Insightful into what?"

"How things work."

"How things work?"

"Insight into the truth, I guess."

"Yes, the truth. That sounds about right. Do you want to hear an interesting idea?"

"Yeah."

"The only seeing to be done in this collective dream of yours is seeing with the heart. Everything essential in life is invisible to our eyes."

"Who said that?"

"That was written by Saint-Exupery," she said.

"The guy who wrote *The Little Prince*?"

"Yes, Dante said the same thing before him in *The Inferno*.

He designated the hottest rings of hell for people who turned a blind eye during a moral crisis—the people who find an excuse to do nothing."

"Do nothing? About what?"

"People who allow circumstance to dictate choice. To turn away from what your heart sees is always the greatest mistake in life."

"Do you believe we go around more than once?"

"Well, it's not really a belief," she said, "it's more like I'm keeping my fingers snugly crossed. I want everything to be fair. It doesn't matter if you're black, white, red, brown, yellow or purple, most sensible people want things to be fair. The majority of people want justice to prevail. That's the most natural proclivity to all humanity. Oh sure, you'll get those who want to muddle things, but we all know it's true, we all just want justice, peace, and happiness. I'm keeping faith this whole thing—our collective dream—is fair. That it all comes out in the wash." She turned to put the magazine in the back seat and saw the book about Edie.

"What's this? How pleasant!"

"What?"

"*I know this book.*" She took it up in her hands. "My Edie! My beautiful little angel!"

"Whaddaya mean?"

"I grew up with Edie over in the valley. We used to ride horses together when we were girls."

"No way!"

"Oh yes, our fathers knew each other. We used to attend their summer and winter parties out on their ranch." She started looking at the pictures. I looked over and saw the one from right before she died, when she was living on De La Vina. It's the 70s and she looks natural and beautiful.

132

"Then she went away to New York," Valerie continued. "We ran into each other one of those years, I think it was her big year—she was in all the magazines. It was Christmas and she was back here visiting her family. We got a coffee and had the most wonderful talk. Then she was back in New York and life went on."

"Wow."

"It was a few years after that, I had been in the hospital for a few months, when we received a new guest to our wing—and it was Edie! She'd been through all her New York City hedonism and was strung out. But she was still there! She was still that beautiful angel!"

"Wow."

"*Oh*, if she was in the mood, she could electrify a room. People wanted to be near her. I remember her, she'd waltz down a hall, perch herself on the lap of some forlorn patient and give them a kiss. I saw how she changed people. She had her dark moments, she was human, but she was special."

There were a lot of coincidences that happened with Edie—I have them written down in a journal somewhere. One was how right around then there was a song about her on the radio. It's a great song too, wistful, the guitar lead awesome. I remember I went out to her grave a handful of times, drank whiskey and played that song with the car doors open. She's buried over in the Santa Ynez Valley.

✻

I had no idea where things were headed. I was getting plastered all the time, smoking grass, cigarettes. And on top of all that I'd started taking stuff home from the pharmacy too—dilaudid and morphine mostly. I was just out of my mind. I was an asshole.

I played music too loud, roommates would ask me to turn it down, and I would, but then sneak it back up a couple notches after a couple songs. For some reason I just couldn't handle head-phones. Everyone wanted to boot me, except this one girl. Her name was Judith. She was this beautiful Jewish girl. She was like twenty-six. She had black, wavy hair, beautiful smooth white skin, and stunning, piercing, slate-blue eyes. She had a boyfriend who put his cigarettes out everywhere. I asked Judith to ask the guy to use an ashtray, and he still did it. I thought it was incredible, until I mentioned it to another roommate.

"Why is that so incredible? We ask you to turn down your stereo all the time, and you don't."

I remember it was a Saturday or Sunday and I was high on something, trying to write poetry, and Judith knocked and asked if I wanted to go down to the beach. She saw I was all messed up. She didn't care. She was pretty unflappable. She was in a bikini top and shorts and she had the raddest body. I wanted her so bad.

On the way down to the beach, that song about Edie came over the radio and I asked if we could crank it. She cranked it. She didn't just turn it up a little, she cranked it. She did it knowing it was what I wanted.

We went down to Butterfly Beach, put down towels and lay in the sun. It was a perfect day, the sun hot enough so you'd go to the water every hour or so.

I came out of the water and got comfortable. I was on a cloud. I felt so calm and peaceful and OK. Morphine is good at that.

Judith is lying there next to me and goes, "Guess what?"

"What?"

"I've been wanting to tell you something."

"Really? Is it good or bad?"

"Well, it's both."

"Let's hear it."

"A few years ago I read a little book. It's called *Drama of the Gifted Child*. It's only about a hundred-and-fifty pages but it contains a really powerful idea. It tells all about what happens if your parent is narcissistic. Do you know what narcissism is?"

"It's when you think the world revolves around you?"

"Yeah, people who do what they want without regard to how it affects someone else."

"Yeah, like when your boyfriend leaves his butts on the boulder by the pond. Or when I get drunk and play music too loud."

"Well, that's part of it. It goes deeper than simply being inconsiderate."

"You think I'm a narcissist?"

"Everyone is to some degree. Narcissism is a part of human nature. Some people are lopsided with it."

"How does someone get to be narcissistic in the first place?"

"It's the opening years of a person's life that are critical. It's in the first five years that the psychic foundation is set. By the time you're five that foundation is either naturally solid, or fractured. Whatever a person's foundation looks like at the end of those five years, the rest of their *life* rests on it."

"OK—first five years—crucial."

"A screwed-up foundation happens by having a parent who is narcissistic—a parent who's had done to them what they're then doing to their child."

"Like that saying," I said, "the sins of the father will be passed to the son."

"Right. But how does the parent cause it in the kid?"

"Yeah—how?"

"Narcissists treat the people around them based on how they feel themselves. If they're feeling good, they treat the people around them good, and if they're feeling bad, they treat the people around them bad. Healthy people do not base the way they treat people on how they're feeling. Now, if you're an adult—a parent—and you act narcissistically to a two- or three- or four-year-old person, this is where the vicious cycle starts. Let's say the parent's feeling bad and the kid does something kids naturally do, craps in their pants or something. The parent freaks out on the kid, maybe even hits him, but he didn't do anything a three-year-old doesn't naturally do. It fractures their self-esteem."

"Their self-esteem?"

"That's what the foundation of a person's life is—their self-esteem. It's the core of who you are emotionally. And if you're screwed up emotionally—"

"You become an adult and start trying to cover up how you feel?"

She told me she thought I was bright but if I never became conscious about certain things about myself I'd never want to stop taking drugs and getting drunk. "You might just end up miserable, making everyone around you miserable," she said.

Shortly after that, Judith moved, I got drunk and cranked the stereo too loud, and the other roommates told me to find another place to live. I got booted from the Castle.

15

So I had to find another place. I found a new ad and called, a European lady answered, and later that night I checked it out. Up behind the Santa Barbara Mission, it was a big, old house built back in 1919. The rules were everyone had to make dinner once a week, and do a few chores each month. There were eight girls and three guys living there. I took a room upstairs the size of a closet.

Two or three nights after moving in I went out with one of the girls living there. Her name was Bridget—she was four or five years older, dark eyes, dark hair, long legs, attractive. She was from a wealthy European family and had a doctorate in philosophy from a university over there. We hit it off.

On the way back up to the place she asked to stop at the mission because she'd never really checked it out. We stopped, looked around for a bit, and got back in the car.

"Hey, you wanna know what?" I said.

"No, what?"

"I think we should mess around."

"Oh really?"

"Yeah. It might be fun."

"Do you think?"

"How does this feel?" I leaned over and gave her a kiss. She liked it.

For the next couple weeks I'd ask her or she'd ask me, and if we both felt like it we'd go to her room or mine and do it. She had the most incredible legs.

I was still taking stuff home from the pharmacy and one day after work I was lying on my bed, junked out, when Bridget knocked on the door. She came in.

"Jack, lying in bed? Are you all right?"

"Yeah. I just feel a little funny, thought I'd lie down." She sat down next to me and stroked my back. I told her it felt good. Someone stroking your back always does.

"I wanted to tell you my sister is coming from Italy."

"I thought you guys were from Austria."

"Her studies are in Italy."

"Where in Italy?"

"In Trieste."

I didn't think about what she said again until a week later, home from work and climbing the front steps, I look up, and there she was—an Edie Sedgwick look-a-like. Short dark hair parted in the middle and hanging close to her face. High cheekbones, little nose, fragile lips. Wearing shorts and a T-shirt, a basket of laundry under her arm, she was headed the other way down the walk.

At dinner, there she was. Bridget introduced us—she went by Renni. She was so hot I had to ignore her all dinner. Besides introductions and a few asides in German to her sister, she didn't say anything.

After dinner everyone went out to the front porch to sit around and have a smoke. There was a cool bunch who lived there. A couple of the older guys and the landlady were an anchor to the place. It was nice to live there.

At one point I was telling everyone this story of how I'd placed an ad in the personals section of the local weekly. I was thinking I needed time and money to write the book, so I thought I'd try and get a wealthy lady to read what I'd written, and if she thought it was going anywhere, she might consider being a patron of the arts. I was always daydreaming about some hot lady I could do it with all night, and then write and do art all day.

There on the steps, I told them about the ad and they laughed and said I was nuts.

"What?" I said, "What if there's some lady out there right now who's lonely and depressed at how boring her life is, and a guy like me might be just the ticket to make her happy? I mean, it could be true." Someone said it was a bold move, and quoted some poet who said that boldness has magic in it.

Renni walked out of the house onto the porch. She was the type that each time you saw her, the further you fell for her. She was electric. Her eyes were very alert.

She pulled a cigar out of her shirt pocket.

"A cigar?" I said.

"Yeah. You want one?"

"Yeah." She pulled a cigar out for me.

"Anyone else?" she asked.

We smoked cigars out front with everyone until it was just her and me left.

"So do you have a boyfriend back in Italy?" I asked.

"No. The boys are afraid of me."

"They're afraid of you? Why?"

"Some months ago a boy I was seeing tried to kill himself."

"Really? Because of you? Because you guys broke up?"

"Yes."

"But he didn't die?"

"No, somebody found him in the woods."

"Somebody found him in the woods? How did he try to do it?"

"He cut his wrist."

*

I got home the next day and saw a motorcycle out front, a 550 trail bike. The landlady said Renni had ridden it home from somewhere. I went to ask her about it.

"How's it goin'?" I said.

"Hi."

"Where'd ya get that bike?"

"It is a friend of Bridget's. He is leaving this to me while I am here."

"He gave you that bike to use while you're here?"

"Yes. Can you ride?"

"Of course, can you?" A 550 is a good-sized bike, and she was slight.

"Oh *p*lease...." To hear her say *oh please* the way she did, I tried to get it out of her whenever I could.

"Seriously—you can ride that?"

"Ohhh, *p-l*ease...."

"If you want I can teach you how to pop wheelies."

"Really?" She actually wanted to know how to do them. She was rad like that. Not every girl wants to know how to do a wheelie.

"Well look, I need to get some beer—you mind if I take the bike down to the store real quick?"

"I want to drink beer," she said. "If you go, you will get me some too, please?"

I remember the horizon glowing a peach-orange color as I rode along Foothill through the warm dry air, the sweet scent of sage and chaparral. That bittersweet sting of nostalgia happened. That same wistfulness.

I got back from getting beer, wrote for a bit, and then got in the shower.

Dinner was served, there was some talk, then a pause.

"So what are you doing up there in your room, Jack— writing?" Renni asked.

"Yeah. Writing, reading."

"What type of writing?"

"Poetry tonight. I got one going right now titled 'Death Song.'"

"What is that about?"

"Well, after the Civil War, back in the 1870s to 1890s, Americans were committing genocide on Native Americans."

"The Indians?"

"Yeah, it's a period known as *the last of the Indian wars*. One episode was in 1872, when a bunch of U.S. troops chased a group of Apaches into a canyon. The Apaches holed up in a cave that had a natural rock wall in front of it. So they're pinned, and there's an occasional shot here and there, arrows shot high, meant to come down on the troops. After a while the troops had an interpreter call out for them to surrender and the Indians told them to go die. The troops couldn't climb the wall without taking losses so a major got the idea to shoot into the cave ceiling and try and ricochet bullets into them. They did and they heard women and children scream. Then they called again for them to surrender and heard nothing until they started to hear this weird chant. The interpreters told the troops to look out—it was the Death Song."

"Oh no," she said.

"Yeah, and then like twenty braves appeared at the wall and started firing down on the troops while some of them tried to get around a flank. But they were shot up and a few of them retreated back. And they continued the Death Song. Then another group of troops got the idea to roll rocks down on them. They did and wiped out the rest, about sixty in all."

"When I was very young, I was given an Indian outfit. As a little girl, I was a Brave."

*

After dinner we all went out to the front porch to have a smoke again. I told more stories about the Indian Wars. There's some really horrible stuff that went on back then. Some ugly things happened all over what is now the United States. Renni was fascinated by it.

Later that night, after we were left alone on the porch again, we started making out. I got her up to my room but I didn't have a rubber and she didn't want to do it without one. I tried to persuade her but it wasn't going to happen, so I gave up and we fell asleep. Then, like at three or four in the morning, she got up and went to the bathroom. The next thing I knew she was kissing the back of my neck to wake me up. She said her period was there so it was OK without a rubber.

As far as having already done it with her sister, Renni didn't care at all—neither of them did. She said they were happy to share me. I was stoked. It was unreal how miserable life had been, and then to be there in Santa Barbara making love with two babes like that.

Bridget, Renni and I were all hanging out together on a Saturday night. We had got back from the bars and were all lying on a bed together. We had candles lit. We were talking about ghosts and they were telling ghost stories. The ghost they'd seen was one their dad had told them he'd seen. He told them it was an ancestor who had originally lived in their big old house out in the country. I didn't have a ghost story. There was a time once where I felt really creepy in some old building down in LA, but I don't know if that was just my imagination or not. I did tell them I'd heard Zaca Lake was haunted by Native American spirits though.

"Zaca Lake?" Renni asked.

"Yeah."

"Indian spirits?" Renni asked.

"Yeah, it was sacred to the Chumash."

"How far away is it?"

"It's over the mountains, back in the valley." Renni sat up, electrified.

"Let's go there right now!"

We made coffee to go, piled in the car with sleeping bags and drove over the mountains. It had been a scorcher back in the valley that day and the air was still warm after midnight. We waded into the lake telling each other to be quiet and swam in the dark.

After we got out we put down our sleeping bags and stared up at the stars. I was reading a lot of folktales that summer and they loved to hear them. One of my favorites is "The Tinderbox."

There's a common soldier. After having been to war and surviving all in one piece, he's on his way home. One night he's walking along a road with his duffle bag and his sword and he comes across a witch. She's really hideous-looking, leaning on a cane. She tells him that the tree there by the side of the road is hollow and has a hole near the top, and if he climbs up there and goes down into it, he can get a whole bunch of money. She says she'll tie a rope around him to get him back out. She goes on to tell him that there's a big tunnel down there, lit with lamps. If he goes down that tunnel, he'll come to three doors. In each room there's a chest with a dog sitting on top of it. If he wants the money in the chest he has to spread the witch's apron on the ground and put the dog on it. In the first room the chest is filled with copper, and the dog's eyes are as large as saucers. In the second room the chest is full of silver, and the dog's eyes are as large as bicycle wheels. In the third room the chest is full of gold, and the dog's eyes are as large as Ferris wheels. "He's quite a dog," she says, "but you mustn't let him stop you."

The solider says that sounds pretty easy and he could use some money, and he asks her what she wants out of it. She tells him she doesn't want anything but this old tinderbox her granny left her. She tells him where it is and she wants him to bring it back with him. So he agrees, the witch gives him the apron, ties a rope around him and away he goes.

He gets down in the tree, goes down the tunnel, and gets to the three doors. He goes into each door and takes all the money he can carry. At the third door, the dog with eyes the size of Ferris wheels kind of freaks him out, but he gets it on the apron, dumps all the copper and silver, and loads his duffle bag with as much gold as he can carry. He grabs the tinderbox, ties the rope around himself, and calls for the witch to pull him out. He gets back out onto the road, asks what she intends to do with the tinderbox, and she cusses him out and tells him it's none of his business. He says she better tell him what she's going to do with it or he'll cut her head off. She asks him who he thinks he is, raises her cane to strike him, and he cuts her head off. He throws the tinderbox into his duffle bag full of gold and heads into town.

He stays at the best places, buys the best of everything, makes lots of friends with the locals, and they tell him about the beautiful princess who lives up in the castle. He asks how he can see her and they all tell him he can't because some fairy said she was supposed to marry some common soldier, so the king and queen have her locked up. He says that's too bad, he would've liked to have seen her.

He goes about having a fine time, going to the theater, the best restaurants. He gives a lot of money to poor people, has a lot of people to help him spend his money, and they all tell him he's wonderful, and he's happy. But he isn't working at anything except spending his money and pretty soon he's running low. Then he runs out and all his friends fall away and he finds himself mending his own shoe in a dingy little apartment one night, when he runs out of light. He goes about looking for a used candle stub when he finds the tinderbox. He knocks on it and the dog with eyes as big as saucers comes out and asks, "What does my master desire?" The soldier tells the dog to go get some money. Bing—the dog's gone—and bang—he's back with a bunch of copper. The soldier figures out that if he hits the tinderbox once, the copper dog appears, twice, the silver dog, and three times, the gold dog.

He gets his old place back and all his friends, and everything is great again, and then one night he starts thinking about the princess. If she's as beautiful as everyone says, he figures beauty is no use if no one sees it. So he knocks on the box, the copper dog appears, and he says, "I'd like to see the princess right away." Bing—the dog is gone to the castle—and bang—he's back with the sleeping princess on his back. The soldier can't believe how beautiful she is. He kisses her, then sends her back to her castle with the dog.

At breakfast the next morning the princess tells the queen she had a dream about a soldier and his dog, that the dog carried her on his back, and the soldier kissed her. The princess thinks it is a beautiful dream and the queen tells her it is disgusting.

The queen wants to find out if it's only a dream or not and has a lady-in-waiting guard the princess that night. Sure enough the soldier has to see her again. The dog goes to get the princess and the lady-in-waiting follows them to the soldier's door. The lady-in-waiting then marks his door with a white cross. When he comes back from dropping the princess off at the castle the dog sees the cross on the door and goes and marks all the other doors in town the same.

Next morning, the king and queen go looking for the soldier but find crosses on every door. The next night, sure enough, the soldier has to see the princess again and the king busts him and throws him into the dungeon. "Tomorrow you'll hang," the king tells him.

The next day they're building the gallows. By the time they finish, everyone is there—the king and queen, the judges and ministers and guards, and everyone from town. The soldier has the rope around his neck and he asks for one last request. He wants one last smoke from his tinderbox. The king asks how he will be able to do that, and the soldier calls out to the audience that he'll give a gold coin to whoever brings him his tinderbox. He tells where it is and some guys from the crowd race to be the one to bring it back. The king and queen are amused. The fastest guy comes back with the tinderbox and it's handed up to the soldier. He thanks the king for granting his request, raps the tinderbox once, then twice, then three times and all the dogs appear. "Quick, I'm about to be hung," the soldier says, "do something." The dogs take all the judges, throw them up into the air and they come screaming down to the ground. Then they take all the ministers, toss them up, and they come screaming down. Then they take the king and queen and do the same and all the guards lay down their weapons.

The soldier asks the princess to marry him, she is pleased and agrees, and they become the new king and queen and everybody rejoices.

*

Then as the summer was drawing to a close, there was a big party over on the Mesa. Everyone from our place went over and it was pretty packed. Loud music, plenty of beer, everyone pink-nosed and sun-bleached. I was in love with Renni, I had fallen for her and I didn't know it. I was crazy about her, I knew that. I just didn't know I'd fallen in love. Her dark-eyed looks, her sounds, her phrases, her cadence—you just always wanted to be around her. And on top of all that, she was just so genuinely fierce for a girl—a tomboy. She'd put on eyeliner at night, but she really would be serious about wanting to learn how to pop a wheelie on a 550—and she did hold one for about ten yards, too. And we went on hikes that summer, and she was a rad hiker, not afraid, so natural on her feet. I was so in love with her and I thought she was into me, but then, at some point during that party she got lost. I couldn't believe it. I saw Bridget and I was like, "Where's Renni?"

"Oh, she went with some other people."

"She went with some other people?" When I heard that my

head got so hot it felt like my ears were melting off. My whole chest was suddenly a big hole that weighed a ton.

A few days later, when it came time to say good-bye at the airport, I was all ruined. We were all teary-eyed, crying for the end of a fun summer. Renni was crying more for the end of the summer, not for me. I could tell.

Then, after she left and I couldn't eat or sleep, I got my license suspended, so I couldn't work for my dad anymore.

Everything was suddenly all wrong again. I ended up on a friend's couch back down in LA.

16

Another friend mentioned a moving company and the next day I found myself in Beverly Hills loading a bunch of expensive furniture onto a truck. The owner wasn't there. One sculpture we moved was a guy in jeans with gay pride graffiti on it. Then I overheard the two guys I was working with, talking.

"What time is Sweet Pants supposed to be here?"

"Anytime."

"Sweet Pants?" I asked.

"Yeah, the owner's houseboy."

"A flamer owns this place," the second guy said. "Faggots have all the money."

"Must've done a lot of suckin' to get a place like this," the first guy said, and they both chuckled.

"Wait till you see where all this shit's going."

"Where?"

"Malibu."

Then we heard the boss downstairs, "Oh! Hello Mr. Collins!"

"It's Mr. Collins," the first guy said.

"Sweet Pants?"

"No, the owner."

I carried a box of stuff downstairs. He was mid-thirties, six feet, fit, with a shock of shiny black hair. He had green eyes, pleasant features. He was an attractive human being.

I went out, loaded the box on the truck, and walking back, he was standing near the front door. He said Hello, and I said Hi back. For the rest of the afternoon he sat near the front door, talked on the phone, and looked through papers. The one other time I looked at him, he was looking at me.

We finished loading the truck and three of us got in the cab to go to the office. I had to sit in the middle.

"Fuckin' fags," the driver said as we climbed in.

"They're goin' to hell," Shotgun said matter-of-factly. "It's just fuckin' sick."

"Who cares?" I said. "It just means more girls for us, right?" They both looked at me like I was an idiot.

The next morning we got in the truck and headed to Malibu.

It was a nice place, ocean view. We start unloading stuff. The owner is there, and near me a lot too. At lunch, when we were all sitting there, one of the guys said, "Yeah, and I think Daddy Sweet Pants has his eye on Jack." Then they made fun for the rest of the day about me getting trapped in the wine cellar with Daddy Sweet Pants.

The next day he got me talking and I told him I was writing a book. He wanted to know all about it and I started thinking he could be a patron. Maybe he could read some of the book and if he thought it was any good, he could provide some space and time for me to finish it.

We met up at Zuma one afternoon.

He gets there with some beer and I tell him about the book, and the Ghost Lady and the Drifter, and how if I only had four walls and some time, I'd be able to finish it. Then he rolls a joint, we get stoned, and it all came out.

"So what are you saying, Jack? You want to be *kept* while you write your book? You want me to get you an apartment?"

"I just want to hand over a few chapters and if you think there's something there, maybe you could be a patron. Or maybe you know someone who might want to be a patron." He didn't say yes or no and asked if I wanted to get some sushi. I thought he meant at a bar, but he meant back at his place.

We got back there, Los Angeles sparkling across the bay, servant in the kitchen making sushi, and it eventually came down to whether I would give it to him or not.

"You've done it with girls there, haven't you?" he asked.

"Yeah."

"What's the difference?"

"There's a difference, but if I do, will you help me so I can get the book done?"

You probably think it's gross, all this, but let me tell you a couple things. First of all, at one of the high schools I went to there was a story going around about a guy on the football team. He was like this star player and his folks were rich and they had a huge place with horses and animals. The story was that sometimes him and his football buddies would get drunk on Saturday night and screw the sheep. They all thought it was hilarious.

Now, alongside that, right around then, I read a quote by some playwright where he said a true artist would steal from their grandma if they had to, to get art made. And I started thinking, if I screw this guy, I can look at it as screwing a sheep to get some art made. Except no animal cruelty or stealing from a grandma. I know it seems ridiculous, but at twenty-one years old that's what went through my mind.

And besides that, I admit, right then I wondered myself. I

don't know if it was because I was so blue about Renni, or what. What if I'd unconsciously brought about the whole situation of being in the gay guy's house in the first place? Maybe my book was a bunch of bullshit. If that was the truth, I wanted to know, and one of the reasons I wanted to know is from something in that chapter, "The Mohawks in High Steel." Besides it telling about what fearless workers the Native Americans were, it told the story of this one guy named John Diabo.

He was the first from his tribe to go to New York City, back in the 1910s. He worked with Irish high steel gangs for a couple months and they all called him Indian Joe. Then a couple of his friends showed up and they started their own gang. One day they were working on Hell Gate Bridge and Diabo fell a couple hundred feet to the river and vanished. His boss said that he was the best of the best and everyone knew it was a freakish accident. He said Diabo must've been a case where he *got in the way of himself*. So being with the handsome gay guy, I wondered if there was something else going on with me. I wanted to find out, I wanted to know. I didn't want to get in the way of myself if that's where my self was headed.

I didn't know what would happen. I found out right there. It's not the most memorable moment of my life, but if you're young and you wonder about it, there's no rule you have to do something. You can abstain from something until you get a clearer picture. And as you get older you might find you were glad to have steered clear of experimenting, or you might find it was the most honest thing you could have done for yourself. It's different for everyone. If it's essential to your wholeness, you'll know. And maybe your feelings will change. It's all dynamic. Straight people go gay, and gay people go straight all the time in this crazy life. It's all dynamic. It really is.

*

I got fired from the moving job because of an argument with the boss. Then through a turn of events I got a job at the Malibu Library, and I was shelving books and there was this one, *The Dictionary of Mythology, Folklore, & Symbols* by Gertrude Jobes. You could look up anything—color, number, letter—and find the symbolism associated with it or just about anything else in reality. You can get lost in it. If you're a little spellbound or a little deluded it could be dangerous.

I have to tell you something else real quick, that happened when I was seventeen. Sometime right before I got my hands on those pills and ended up in the hospital.

I can't remember what I'd read that sparked my interest, but it made me want to find out about Cabala. Cabala is ancient Jewish mysticism that Madonna and a lot of Hollywood stars are into. I don't know what their understanding is, but when I was younger I saw it mentioned somewhere. I went to the library, picked out some books, and reading an introduction, the author, a rabbi, said there were people who thought it was wrong that he'd written what he had. That once you heard the knowledge he was going to tell, you weren't supposed to talk about it. I closed the book. I didn't want to read anything I couldn't talk freely about. If I read anything like that, I'd spill the beans for sure. I didn't want trouble. I returned it. But from then on though, I kept an eye open when Cabala was mentioned in whatever I was reading. Whenever I saw it, I studied it, whatever the context was.

Now fast forward a few years later, and there I was working at the library. And in that dictionary of mythology, folklore, and symbols, at the end of a description of a particular number, it told its value cabalistically. For instance, twenty-one, in high form—a love of abstract science, art, and poetry. In low form, ignorance.

There were other things besides numbers that said what

something meant cabalistically, and from dipping into that dictionary, I started to figure this secret knowledge, this mysticism, is based on a divination by numerology. That every letter had a numerical value, which meant every word did, so you could assign value to anything in reality—and from there—if you were some kind of wizard or something—you could interpret reality. No way I was ever going to be a wizard, but that's what I found out about that stuff.

Then they had to let me go from the library because I was taking too long to shelve books, and I got a job at a deli across the street—which was good—because I got to take home food.

"Hey dude, what's up?"

"Not much."

"Can I crash on the couch tonight?"

"What kind of food you got?"

*

But I had delusions of grandeur going on. I didn't know what it was then, but I was convinced I had something to say, and it was going to be great, and therefore I was already great. Just like sexuality is dynamic a lot of the time, so is sanity.

Then I read in the *Malibu Times* about a local homeless guy who thought he was Jesus. I'd seen him around. When I saw the article, I was like, Oh that guy. He always wore white. For being homeless he did a remarkable job keeping his clothes clean. I remember passing him on the way to hitchhike through the canyon once, asked if he wanted food, and gave him some. He may not have been Jesus, but he was enlightened in some way for sure. Either that, or it was a really strong act. And, as the saying goes, whatever it is you want to become, just start acting like it—practice whatever you have to practice and eventually it might happen.

17

Then a room opened up at a friend's house and I moved in. It had a pool table in the garage and most the guys who stopped over to drink beer and shoot did construction, so I quit the deli and picked up day jobs while I worked on the book. I could work for two or three days and then write for a week—even longer if there was a good parade with big crowds on the weekend.

Right around then, while trying to climb out of the abyss of getting over Renni, and quitting drugs and sobering up, I was having a melt-down with the book. Trying to get the Ghost Lady to come to life, getting the Drifter to be solid and whole, I'd read an old chapter and wonder who the heck I thought I was kidding. Work I'd combed over for hours and hours, sometimes I'd look at it and see nothing but trash. It was incredibly depressing—suicide crossed my mind more than once.

Although I was doing it on my own, pulling my own weight, I was basically a basket case. There were a few guys around who still believed in me, but for the most part I scared the hell out of everyone, all whacked out on my unconscious.

Then I tried sales again, and after going the whole night without a single sale, I walked to the on-ramp to hitchhike out of the valley and this guy picked me up in a work truck. His name was David—a contractor of some sort—tools in the back, a Milwaukee Sawsall on the floor. He was one of those contractors with blueprints and papers and receipts all over the place. He was a big white guy. He looked like a big Jim Morrison.

"What kind of work are you doing?" I asked.

"Masonry."

"You're a contractor?"

"Yeah."

"Been doin' it long?"

"My dad was a mason. I always tell people I've been doing it ever since I was old enough to pick up a brick."

"I've done construction. I'm doin' door-to-door sales right now." He asked what kind and I told him about the car maintenance deal. "I just zeroed tonight," I said, "didn't even make a sale."

"Well, I happen to need some help for a new job. Can you get down to PCH about eight in the morning?"

"Sure."

We stopped at the red light at the off-ramp at Las Virgines. It's one of those off-ramps where if you pull ahead a little, or close to the line, the guy behind can get past for a right-hand turn. As he fished for a card through papers on the front seat, another truck pulled up behind us and laid on the horn. Some beefy construction guy stuck his head out the window—"Move your fucking truck!" David looked back at the guy. "Look," he said, "can't find a card. If you want to work, be on the south-east corner of Webb and PCH at eight, Tuesday."

"I'll be there," I said, and right before I shut the door, a thermos fell to the ground. It bounced and rolled under his truck. I looked at him like, Sorry. The light turned green. "No problem," he said and put the truck in park. I had to get on a hand and knee to get the thermos, as the guy behind us laid on the horn again. Then I saw David's work boot step onto the asphalt. I stood up with the thermos in time to see them both out of their trucks headed towards each other. They were both big guys, but the other guy was beefy, and yelling, "You stupid motherfucker!" Right at the critical distance, the beefy guy threw a punch. David bobbed out of the way like a pro boxer, and stepping back into it, landed a stiff right to the chin. Boom—out went the lights. The guy dropped to his knees with glazed eyes. Falling forward, David grabbed him by the neck, sidestepped to the curb, and shoved him onto the dirt. I tossed the thermos in the truck, he got back in and he made the turn into the canyon.

*

I got there Tuesday morning, he picked me up and we headed south.

"If you don't mind me asking, where'd you learn to punch like that?"

"Well, I told you my dad was a mason, right?"

"Yeah."

"Well, he was a boxer too. I used to box." He mumbled something about golden gloves.

I started working for David every day. He wouldn't let you call him Dave—I heard him correct other contractors more than once. He was from Ohio, about thirty-five, and no-nonsense. He could smile and laugh, but was pretty stoic most of the time. I'd told him I was writing a book and on the way to jobs I'd tell installments of the story.

He had all the really nice jobs—Pacific Palisades and Malibu—big houses. I learned what brick tongs were and how to mix up a wheelbarrow full of mortar.

After a few weeks and a couple different jobs, at the end of one day he told me to meet him at the north-west corner at ten instead of eight.

The next morning I got a ride through the canyon right away, had some time, and went to the bookstore to look at books. I saw one about the 60s. I wanted to see if there was anything about Edie in it. There was—one of the NYC pictures. I started reading how she was the subject of some Bob Dylan songs. I never really got Dylan. "Lay Lady Lay" is good. What Hendrix did with "All Along the Watchtower" is unreal. "Knockin' on Heaven's Door" is good. That song is in the movie *Pat Garret and Billy the Kid*. Dylan is actually in the movie too—he plays this quirky, knife-thrower guy. I think that movie is the best western ever shot. Peckinpa directed it. I wouldn't be surprised if he told Kris Kristofferson to play Billy the Kid like Morrison as a cowboy. The inflections and cadence of his voice—there's one scene when Billy the Kid kills a couple sheriffs who'd tried to capture him, and while he's breaking off his leg chains, he goes into this rap just like Morrison might've—he even says *marijuana* in the middle of it.

Anyway, David picks me up and instead of going south on PCH, we go north.

"Where we going?"

"Somewhere around Point Dume."

The thought crossed my mind that it was going to be the gay guy's house, and for a few minutes my mind raced and I got worried and wouldn't have been surprised at all to have the past come back and haunt me—but it wasn't.

The property was an awesome few acres of the Santa Monica Mountains. There was a long dirt road that went up along a creek to an old, wooden guard house. We got to it and a Mexican guy greeted us. On the inside of the guardhouse I noticed, pinned up, were all these Polaroids of hippie types. A guy with a jug of wine, a few different babes, most of them pretty stoned-looking. I couldn't figure it out, why were there Polaroids of all these scrubby-looking people pinned to the inside of this little rickety guardhouse?

We got out of the truck and David told me to hang tight till he got back. Him and the other guy walked back into the property. Out where I was, there was a small field before some chaparral going up a hillside. Then I heard something. I couldn't make out what it was but I heard where it came from and went there. It was a metal cage trap and in it was a reddish-grey fox. He saw me as I approached and bared his pointy little teeth, and made—it's hard to describe the sound a caged fox makes. Kind of like a hissing fox growl. It was weird.

When David and the guy got back, I told the guy there was a fox in the trap. Then David wanted to see it so all three of us checked it out for a minute.

The whole day we dug the trenches and poured the footings. I always liked to draw things in the fresh cement and before we left I took a nail and drew a Native American thunderbird symbol.

✻

The next day we got there and David told me to wait down in the field again while he went and talked to the owner. I went over to check the fox trap and the little guy was still in there. When David got back and we started getting ready to work, I asked if the

Mexican guy was going to let it go.

"I don't know," he said.

"Isn't that cruelty to animals?"

"I don't know."

"How many days would you let go by before mentioning something?"

"Maybe tomorrow, maybe the next day."

"Why wait so long?"

"Because *one*, it's none of my business, and *two*, I don't know what the owner has planned. Maybe he's learned that if he leaves the fox in the trap for a few days, when he finally let's it out, it doesn't come back."

The footings were ready to be built on, the thunderbird symbol came out good, and I started unloading bricks while David laid out lines. Then I got the mortar ready and we started building.

"What's this going to be for?"

"I think it's going to be a rose garden."

"There's a huge rose garden in my book," I said. "It's where some of the scenes take place."

"Oh yeah?"

"Yeah, it's the rose garden where the Ghost Lady goes when she's all upset about not being able to leave the mansion."

"Why can't she leave the mansion?"

"Because she's cursed, because of what happened."

"Because she got it on with the Drifter?"

"The curse is from the *original* drifter, back when the Ghost Lady was still alive in the flesh."

"So, there's a drifter that rides into town when she's a young woman and still alive?"

"Right."

"And they get it on, she gets pregnant and then dies with birth?"

"Right."

"And your story starts when the second drifter rides into town, years after what happened between the young woman and the first drifter?"

"Right."

"And it's the second drifter that gets it on with her when she's the Ghost Lady, and somehow that lifts the curse?"

"Right."

"How does he get it on with a ghost?"

"I don't know, he just does—and she's not really a *ghost*—she's a spirit."

"Oh."

"It's probably a metaphor for something, I don't have it all figured out yet."

"I like it, I think it's good."

*

David asked about Jung quite a bit. I told him everything I knew. Basically, let me try and finish up the Jungian stuff here. I have to tell you this otherwise, later, when I get to the conclusion—and there is a conclusion—I promise—the whole thing won't make sense. I've got a few more stories to go before I can put all the pieces together, but I just want to get to the last of the Jungian stuff here.

*

There's one archetype Jung identified that I mentioned, called the Shadow archetype. Like the Hero archetype, it's pervasive all through life and art. The Joker in the Batman stories is a great shadow archetype. In Native American folklore they call the shadow the Trickster, usually a coyote. The shadow is the part of the person that could be added to the personal consciousness but for various reasons isn't. It's kind of a paradox because it's the side of yourself that you're blind to, but like a sparring partner, it helps you see what you've been unaware of. If you're totally unconscious of your shadow, all you do is go around projecting it onto other people, stuff like, "That guy is an asshole!" A lot of the time when someone says something like that they're really just talking about themselves.

But because to go around projecting yourself, unaware, is a lame way to live, to become whole you have to face your shadow, you have to become conscious of stuff you don't want to. It's not easy. That's what Jung thought the dilemma of modern Christianity was—that Christians were taught to reject the part that's animal in nature—the bodily desires.

Anyway, there's this saying—To the darkness doomed those who worship only the body, and to the darkness doomed those who worship only the spirit—but to those who worship both— through the body overcome death, and through the spirit achieve immortality.

*

So I told David all that stuff and he goes, "Well Jack, I have to tell you, these ideas are all really interesting. I like the idea that human beings have things in common, these archetypes, things that bridge cultural differences. I like that," he said. "I've always thought that to be true—that no matter your color or culture—there's common ground where all human beings are equal. But one question that keeps coming back to me is, does any of this show you how to live?"

"Whaddaya mean?"

"Does it provide you with a philosophy on the correct way for a human being to approach existence?"

I had to think about that for a second. "There is no correct way," I said. "Everyone's operating on the information they've individually processed. How can there be a correct way to live with each person's life made up of so many different things? With all the different people in the world, and different levels of intelligence and opinions—the idea that there's a correct way to live? *No way.*"

"Are you sure?"

"Yeah. The only correct way to live is to not do things that will kill you, and to stay out of people's business. That's the correct way to live? Right?"

"Why do jets fly?"

"Why do jets fly? Because they have wings attached to an engine."

"Right. So is it true that wings can be designed to cause lift?"

"Yeah."

"And it's true that a set of wheels will get you from one city to the next a lot quicker than walking?"

"True."

"And if you pour wine into a glass that has a hole, the wine will leak out?"

"Yeah."

"And if you drink too much beer or wine, you puke?"

"Right."

"So, you don't think all those truths, and all the others you could sit around for hours and think up—you don't think all those truths add up to one giant truth?"

I thought about it for a while and somehow made the distinction that there had to be two sets of truth—truths in the physical realm—wings, wheels, and puking—and truths in the realm of opinion.

"There have to be two sets of truth," I said. "Those applied to the physical world, and those applied to opinion."

"You're right," he said.

"But doesn't that contradict the idea that there's a correct way to live? Because what if I think pineapple on pizza sucks, and you don't—who's correct?"

"A correct way to live, and a correct way to enjoy life are two different things. It's not whether someone is correct about pineapple, it's whether someone is correct about their diet. Should you eat pizza morning, noon, and night?"

"OK, there's a correct way to approach diet."

"Since the universe is always transforming, and our physical bodies are set in the center of that equation—and it's always been that way—we're participating in it, but it's ultimately out of our control—don't you think that after a while mankind would figure out the best way to approach that circumstance? If the universe is transformation and life is opinion, and that's the way it's always been—"

"So there's a correct way to live?"

"Yep."

"What is it?"

"The core idea?"

"Yeah."

"The core idea is that there are only two things in life—those you can control, and those you can't."

"That's the core principle of the correct way to approach existence?"

"Yep. You can't control the universe, or what other people think or feel—all you can control is yourself."

"I mean, that's so simple though."

"Well, there're people driving down PCH right now, really worried about things totally out of their control."

"It must be hard to live with that in mind—throughout the day I mean—approaching everything on the basis of whether it's in or out of your control or not."

"It gets easy with practice."

"So who came up with this idea? The Chinese?"

"It shows up in different places, and in different parts of the world too."

"Who told you all this?"

"My father."

"Your dad was a boxer, and he read books?"

"Yep."

"So who thought of it first, the idea?"

"The Taoists came up with the oriental version in the East, and the Stoics came up with the occidental version in the West. You figure if two cultures from opposite sides of the world came to the same conclusion, it's got to be a pretty big idea."

"Yeah."

"Want to hear a Taoist fable?"

"Sure."

"There was a farmer who had a wife, son, and a single horse to plow their field.

"One day the horse jumps the fence. The farmer's neighbor comes over, is told what happened, and goes, 'Oh, that's bad—that's bad.' And the farmer replies, 'Who knows what's good or bad?'

"A week later, the horse who ran away had become the leader of a small herd. He comes back with the other horses and now the farmer has a few. The neighbor comes over, is told what happened and goes, 'Wow, that's good—that's good.' And the farmer goes, 'Who knows what's good or bad?'

"About a week after that, the farmer's son, breaking in one of the new horses, gets bucked and snaps his leg. The neighbor comes over, is told what happened and goes, 'Oh, that's bad—that's bad.' And the farmer goes, 'Who knows what's good or bad?'

"A week later, the army comes along, conscripting for a war, but the son doesn't have to go because his leg's busted."

"So let me get this straight," I said. "There are only two things in life—those you can control, and those you can't. And it's stupid to worry about things that aren't in your control, and things that might appear to be bad might really end up being good."

"Right."

"So doesn't that mean it's stupid to worry about anything?"

"No. It means you should never worry about anything but yourself—what you say and what you do—because here in reality, that's all you have control over."

*

Still working on that brick thing in the rose garden, one morning we got there and when I got out of the truck I found a peacock feather. I'd seen a couple around before but none that were perfect. There was no dust on it, all the iridescent blues, and greens, and purples and pinks. I put it in the cab of the truck, and when I got home I pinned it to my wall.

The next day we got there to finish and I had to go up near the house to get something. The rose garden was down in a lower part of the property. I'd never seen the owner.

Anyway, I was getting something when I heard a screen door slap shut. I looked over and there's this white guy with brown-gray hair that looked like a giant beehive wrapped up around his head. He'd just woken up or something and had a coffee mug in his hand. I happened to look over when it happened. He must've been barefoot because all of a sudden he jumped onto one foot the way you do when you step on something sharp. And in doing that, he spilled coffee all down his bathrobe. He stood there a second, checked himself out, then went back in the house.

I got back down to David and told him what I just saw.

"You know who that was?" he asked.

"No. Who?"

"Bob Dylan."

18

I got really good at mixing up a wheelbarrow full of cement, getting the right amount of water on first try. At the end of the day I came back to my room dirty and beat, but I was making more than just rent working like that.

Things were going pretty good and one day David and I were getting lunch at John's Garden, the sandwich shop there in Malibu. It was one of those perfect days, sun blazing, a south swell of waves pumping. I was telling David about days just like it from my past. I told him about a day when I was seventeen. A few of us had finished lunch, and headed back, someone wanted to get something out of Market Basket. So the rest of us are leaning against the side wall, passing a joint around or something, when all of a sudden I notice this tall, thin guy come into view from around the storefront corner. He's all distraught, gesturing, running his hand through his hair, and he notices us. He comes over going, "I can have a Coke if I want—right?" It was some artist or celebrity, but I couldn't figure out who he was. "I can if I want—right?" he said again. "Someone told me I can't buy a Coke! This is insane! This has gone too far!"

"You can buy a Coke if you want," someone said. We even offered to go buy it for him, but right then a big, black Mercedes pulled up and some guy got out. "Brian! Brian, c'mon. We gotta go, Brian!" Then they both got in the car and took off.

After a few minutes we figured out it was Brian Wilson. For the rest of the day, out in the water, we were like, "That was Brian Wilson!" Turning around to paddle into a wave the size of a house, "It's gone too far! You cannot—you will not—buy a Coke!" We sang the Beach Boys at the top of our lungs. The waves were so good that day.

I had just finished telling David about all that, and we were finishing up lunch, when someone tapped me on the shoulder. It was Goddess Lady!

"Hey—what's up?!" We gave each other a hug and I introduced David to her. They shook hands and if sparks can fly between two people, it happened between them.

"Hey," she said to me. "Remember a while ago when I told you I was going to read up on the Sumerians? The stuff about the Greek gods and Noah being in the same story?"

"Yeah?"

"Well, I finally got around to it. I've been meaning to call you, can we talk over the phone tonight?"

"Yeah."

Then she said it was good to see me, told David it was nice to meet him and left. David and I went back to work and he never stopped asking questions about her the rest of the day. I was worried. Seeing her, and how hot she was, if she wasn't into me the way I was into her, I didn't want to go through feeling blue again. I'd rather take a beating or sit in a dentist's chair than feel that way—that hole in your heart that weighs a ton. That desire to be with someone as much as someone can want to, and not be— ugh!

She called and we caught up on everything and I asked if she was still with her boyfriend and she said, "Kinda." I was just about to feel good about the possibilities, but then she started asking about David and I got hit with heartache. It killed me when I heard she was into him. It didn't hurt quite as much as it *could have* because they were the same age and looked like they should be together. They really did make a good-looking couple. Talking to her on the phone reminded me of when we were together. I started getting blue.

"So," I said, "what did you find out about the Sumerians?"

"What if I told you there's an idea out there that makes the *Old Testament* of the Bible and the theory of evolution both true at the same time?"

"That would be rad."

"If someone came up to you on the street and asked whether you were a Creationist, or an Evolutionist, what would you say?"

"Can evolution be part of creation?"

"Let me rephrase it," she said. "If someone asked if you believed life randomly evolved or was intelligently designed, what would you say?"

"I don't know."

"OK. I just finished reading a book, and the only reason it came to be written was because of this Jewish kid named Zechariah. He was studying the *Old Testament* one morning and he read something in *Genesis*. Most people know *Genesis* is about the creation of the world, and the Garden of Eden, and Adam and Eve, but there's a lot more going on in that book besides that."

"Like what?"

"Well, after Adam and Eve have to leave the garden because they ate from the tree of knowledge, they have to go live by the sweat of their brow, right?"

"Right."

"Then it says that when it came to pass that men began to multiply on earth, and they had daughters—*that the sons of God saw the daughters of men were fair.*"

"What does that mean?"

"It means the sons of God started getting it on with the daughters of men," she said.

"Who were the sons of God? You mean *angels?*"

"That's what Zechariah wanted to know. Who were they? They weren't human, but they were getting it on with the female humans? Verse four of chapter six calls them giants. In the original Hebrew their name means, *those who from above came down.*"

"Those who from above came down?"

"Yeah," she said. "Zechariah asked his teacher about them, wasn't satisfied with the answer, and set out on a lifelong mission to find out who they were. He graduated from college and over decades became a scholar of Near East studies. He knew Latin, Greek, Phoenician, Sanskrit, and finally—the oldest known writing—Cuneiform."

"Cuneiform?"

"It's the oldest known writing to mankind, lines of little wedge-shaped characters stuck into clay tablets."

"And it's way older than Hebrew? Written before the Bible?"

"Way before the Bible—way before Egyptian hieroglyphics even."

"So what does this cuneiform writing have to do with making science and the Bible true at the same time?"

"About a-hundred-and-fifty years ago," she said, "in the 1800s, the French and British went back to Mesopotamia to excavate, and over the years, slowly but surely, we've uncovered all the layers of civilization—from the Greeks, back to the Phoenicians and Canaanites, the Babylonians and Assyrians, to the Akkadians, and all the way back to the oldest known, the Sumerians. They finally found Eridu, the first Sumerian city according to all the olden texts, and underneath it, nothing but virgin soil. "

"Cool," I said.

"And not only was it the oldest civilization, but after examining all the records, scholars found it was more advanced than civilizations that followed it. To this day official science has no idea how or why Sumerian civilization appeared. All of a sudden there was first use of the wheel, writing and mathematics, weights and measures, knowledge of pi, astronomy, laws and courts, medicine, agriculture and animal husbandry, beer and wine, beekeeping— all this stuff—everything we equate with high civilization—and everything ours rests on today—and it appeared as if out of nowhere."

"OK," I said. "Sumerians, oldest civilization, cuneiform, oldest known writing—so where does the Bible come in?"

"It turns out that the Sumerian writings are the most complete when it comes to the creation story. Guess how many chapters it takes *Genesis* to describe the creation of earth, and Adam and Eve?"

"How many?"

"*Three*. That's it. The world, Adam and Eve, and the whole animal kingdom are up and running by the end of chapter *three*. The Sumerian version—the first and original version of the *same* story—is *hundreds* of chapters. The book of *Genesis* is like a whole novel hacked down to a page-and-a-half. The Judeo-

Christian culture has been interpreting reality based on a few phrases from a book that was originally *thousands* of phrases."

"And the original version is where Adam and Eve, and Zeus and Hera and Apollo and Athena are all in the same story?"

"Yeah."

"How?"

"First—what do you know about evolution? If someone walked up to you on the street and asked for a rough timeline of the evolution of human beings, what would you say?"

"Well," I said, "that sea creatures eventually moved onto land, and after millions and millions of years, the land creatures evolved into apes, and then the apes evolved into Neanderthals, and we evolved from them. Right?"

"More or less, yeah. At a certain point we went from apes who went across the ground on all fours, to walking on two feet like we do today. We became *homo erectus*. Hominids."

"Then what?"

"Then after a while an advanced hominid figured out how to bang two rocks together to make a sharp edge—and for two million years—from the advanced hominid all the way to Neanderthals—the tools of these two groups—sharp stones— were alike—and both as they appeared physically were hardly distinguishable."

"OK."

"And then there was this unexplainable progression where we acquired a fifty-percent increase in brain size, our face became flat, and we slipped into an utterly changed, modern anatomy. Darwinism has always failed miserably to explain this. Current science implies we've discovered the *missing link*. Even if that was the case, of the random mutation and natural selection that would have to had taken place, almost simultaneously and so perfectly, over such a short period of time—even if there was fossil evidence linking us to Neanderthals, it still doesn't explain how such a change happened in the blink of an eye—there's just *no way.* And on top of all the sudden and unexplained changes in our features, guess what else came along?"

"What?"

"Fire and Art—and all of a sudden we go from using sharp stones to specialized tools of wood and bone. So the question is, how is it that after two million years of being naked apes, did we suddenly become these lithe and hairless creatures who know how to utilize fire and start painting depictions of ourselves and our existence on cave walls?"

"Is there an answer?"

"Yes."

"It's in the cuneiform?"

"Yes—we were created."

I listened to her and then started going to the library a lot.

Of all the facts, and all the evidence from every field of science, it seems that what the Sumerians said about us—humanity—is the truth. Now, the stuff I'm about to tell you can be refuted—no doubt about that—I'm not claiming it's indisputable. All I'm saying is that it could be the truth, and if it is, and we're not allowed to talk about the truth, then it would follow that it would meet with a lot of resistance. And it does. I've been researching and discussing this for a while now, and I know what the so-called experts have to say, and I know what the latest in science has to say, and all I can say is, that there's a lot of information that points to it being the truth. So I can only relate to you what I see, and if you don't see it, I'm sure you'll find it interesting anyway.

The story is, that a long time ago, *those who from above came down* landed here. The reason they came was to mine gold and silver because Earth had a lot of it.

The mining operation went along, but at some point the captain and chief science officer decided they were going to create a worker—a *lulu* they called it. They took Neanderthal DNA, mixed it with some of their own DNA, and created us—humans. They bioengineered us to be their workers and pets. Two brothers were in charge of the whole operation, Enlil and Enki. Their names have changed over the centuries—they became known as Zeus and Poseidon—and then eventually as God and the Serpent, but in the original version they were called Enlil and Enki. And Enlil outranked Enki, just like Zeus outranked Poseidon, and God outranked the Serpent.

The story is, Enlil thought that because *they* had bioengineered *us*, that we should never know what we really are. But Enki thought that because we had consciousness just like they did, that we should know we're gods, just like them. That if we were told the truth, with time, we might become as great as them—maybe even greater. That's why he told Eve to eat the apple and give some to Adam, so we'd become conscious and know the difference between good and evil. Which means that no particular type of being is God, but that *Consciousness* is God.

Things went along the way Enlil wanted, and humans back then, thousands of years ago, were like domesticated animals. We built them their palaces, and raised the cattle, and harvested the crops, and made the wine. Sumerian and Akkadian texts tell how the gods were able to ascend into the heavens and roam earth's skies at will. The cuneiform texts use words like *sky chamber, celestial boat that gives off light, fire-bird of stone*. Back then the gods had aircraft and were flying all over the place, visiting each other in their little Shangri-Las we built for them. At one point while excavating Mesopotamia, archaeologists found a life-sized statue of a woman decked out in flight gear. I've seen the photos—four thousand years old, some hot looking astronaut babe with a helmet and flight suit. I swear, it's true.

According to the Sumerians there was a pantheon of twelve gods that ruled a bunch of lesser gods who were all flesh and blood like us. They had figured out how to manipulate their own DNA and they lived for hundreds of years and they were all part of a big, but not necessarily peaceful, family. And we recorded the tales of their ascents and descents between heaven and earth, and all their friendships and rivalries, and marriages and infidelities. But after a while, like it says in the Bible, pretty soon some of the gods started getting it on with the humans. And that was when Enlil told everyone that the experiment with the lulus—us—was over. They knew how to manipulate the weather, and the plan was to wipe us out with a flood.

There was a huge argument about it, and a bunch of yelling and crying, but in the end they all had to swear they wouldn't tell us the end was coming. Except Enki. He figured he was going to give us one shot to survive. He went and found the most righteous guy he could, took him aside and said, "Look, I've sworn by all the gods not to tell any human this information. So, I want you to stand behind that wall of reeds and listen to everything I say to myself." And he goes on to tell the guy that a flood is coming, that he's got to build a boat, and everyone is going to think he's crazy, but he's got to get it together—and fast.

You can see how the same stories got told and retold down through the ages, each time with less information, until to the point today, where we treat Zeus and Poseidon and Noah as myth when maybe they're just remnants of what really happened. If it's true, if there really was an advanced form of us who landed here and then bioengineered us, the most obvious question is, are they still here? And if they're not, are they ever coming back?

19

Goddess Lady wanted to meet David again. I told her we always went to John's Garden for lunch. She showed up and I said I had to go get an espresso or something and left them alone. A few nights later I called her kind of buzzed and asked if they had gone out. She said they did. David never mentioned it but he was getting it on with her.

I kept working with him and just kind of tried to think of it like the farmer whose horse runs off—*who knows what's good or bad?* Then David got news his dad was sick, and then his sisters were having a hard time taking care of things and he had to go back to Ohio for a while. When I found out, I called Goddess Lady again and she said she was going with him.

"I don't know if I'll be able to handle living out there or not," she said. "I'm just going to take things one day at a time."

Before they left, David gave me some numbers I could call for work and that was the last I saw or heard from either of them.

*

I called the numbers for work and one guy had a job refinishing the bar and some booths in a restaurant. He gave me the address and it turned out it was the Hard Rock Cafe down on Beverly and San Vicente. If you've ever been there then you know how they have a whole bunch of rock n' roll memorabilia all over the place. Above the bar they had a bunch of guitars from different rock stars—Elvis, Hendrix, Richards. They had John Lennon's guitar from the Beatles' first tour. Of all the guitars, if I was going to say I played one, I wanted to play Lennon's most. During a break, when no one was around, I took it down, tuned it, and played some bar chords. I wished I knew a Beatles' song.

A couple days after that I was in a library and ran into the *Playboy* book of interviews. I checked it out and there were two with Lennon.

At one point in an interview from 1981, Lennon goes off on the Rolling Stones and questions why they're still together, and that it's silly. "In the Eighties," he says, "they'll be asking, 'Why are those guys still together?'"

To tell you the truth, Lennon sounds kind of lame throughout a lot of the interview. Yoko's in it, she sounds lame too. They say some good stuff though. Like where he's asked about Neil Young's lyric that it's better to burn out than to fade away, he says it's a bunch of bullshit making Hendrix or Morrison or Sid Vicious a hero—that he idolizes people who survive. And Yoko says stuff about the importance of family and relationships—the jumping-off point though, is her talking about how important it was for her to take over their $150,000,000, and how important it was for him to stay home and be a house-husband. In the interview it seems like doing whatever she wanted made him happiest—like she could've said, "Go ahead, continue making music with them," and he would've been just as happy. At one point she mentions how the Beatles were a medium, not really conscious of what was coming through them but that the spirit of the era used them. Lennon says, "Whatever wind was blowing at the time moved the Beatles too. I'm not saying we weren't flags on top of a ship, but the whole boat was moving. Maybe the Beatles were in the crow's-nest, shouting 'Land-ho,' or something like that, but we were all in the same damn boat."

When the interviewer asks whether they'll reunite to do a benefit for charity, Lennon says it's all a rip-off. "I am not going to get locked into that business of saving the world on-stage," he says. "The show is always a mess, and the artist always comes off badly." What a crock, I thought. It's not about *saving* the world *John*, it's about *helping* the world. The only way an artist can come off badly is if they have motives other than helping.

Then the interviewer asks about Bangladesh, the concert where Harrison and Dylan and others performed, and he goes, "You'll have to check with Mother, because she knows the ins and outs of it, I don't. But it's all a rip-off. So forget about it." If anything, the interview points out how incredible the influence of one person can be on another in a relationship—how if someone was with someone else they'd be a completely different person.

There's another interesting part in the interview where, of Beatles' songs, John says a lot of his stuff is "the middle eight," the bridge. Like, he tells how Paul walks in one day and is singing the first few bars to "Michelle" and doesn't know where to go with it and Lennon suggests: "I *love* you, I *love* you, I *l-o-o-ve* you...." And one part I really zeroed in on is where they're talking about LSD and he goes into how he ended up "getting the message" to destroy his ego with acid. "Bit by bit over a two year period, I had destroyed me ego," he says. "I didn't believe I could do anything. I was just nothing. I was shit." Then a friend took him aside and told him he was all right, and pointed out which songs he had written. "You wrote this, and you said this, and you are intelligent, don't be frightened." Then Lennon tells how he "started fighting again, being a loudmouth again and saying, 'I can do this. Fuck it.'"

Then, after talking about LSD and more about the Beatles, Lennon goes, "This Beatles talk bores me to death. Turn to page 196." He meant it as a joke, knowing the interview was going to be in print. In the actual book of *Playboy* interviews though—more than 700 pages—page 196 happens to be the 1966 interview with Timothy Leary, and that particular page mentions LSD like fifty times!

But, about Lennon, not only did he create arguably the most definitive song of western civilization—"Imagine"—and not only did he go through periods in his life where he was full of shit, he was still right about a lot of things. You can go back to those interviews and read them and see he really was a genius. He was. He was dead wrong about the Rolling Stones though.

20

I was about to close the book of *Playboy* interviews, but checked the contents to see who else was in there and I saw the name of a writer Beautiful Halloween Girl's dad had mentioned. An American writer named Gore Vidal. He writes about the presidents a lot. He's a scholar of American history. There was this one essay he wrote and the entire thing was about four words—a secret phrase—buried in the U.S. Constitution.

I remembered what Beautiful Halloween Girl's dad said about the 1947 National Security Act and how it was the seed that grew into the military/industrial complex, and how that was the thing keeping the whole mess—our whole ridiculous approach to existence—from being cleaned up. Then, when I found out what was written on those Sumerian tablets, I always kept a lookout for anything that might solve the problem. I mean, however this big fake show and all the phoniness is orchestrated—controlling things with bread and circus, and divide and rule—and all the misery from a never-ending war on *terror*—how can that be good? Jealous gods, or slimy humans, or a combo—whoever or whatever —the point is—benefiting the few at the expense of the many is *morally wrong*. That's why poets have always said all of history is a moral drama, because there's always going to be people having to make tough decisions between right and wrong. The people who want to keep things the way they are will ask, How do you know what's right or wrong? Who are you to judge?

I was in a coffee shop once, and I got in a conversation with this guy—thinning hair, dandruff, pot-bellied—average old white guy—and we're talking about how bogus the latest war is.

"So how do we even know what's right or wrong, anyway?" I asked.

"*Harm*," he said. "Harm is the prerequisite to reasoning about what is right or wrong. Harm is the only proper measure of value."

"Can something be wrong without harm?"

"If you want to argue an act can be wrong without harm, those positions have to do with emotion in judgment. People have moral convictions, which can be dangerous because we might condemn actions, and even people, we have no good reason to."

"So sometimes moral judgments are nothing more than saying—hurray for my team!"

"Sometimes. But you can't assume emotion has no role to play in moral reasoning. Would a torturer torture if they were able to put themselves in the place of their victim? Atrocities are possible because people's moral emotions have been switched off. A moral conviction is valid when you can show the harm caused. That's how we know torture and rape and murder are morally wrong."

Someone once said that the ugliest thing about seeking the truth is that you'll find it. That's what things come down to today—either you want to know the truth or you don't. You *do* or you *don't*. There's no wanting to know only *half* the truth—not if you've got a spine at least.

Well, no matter how ugly or bizarre, I'm the type that wants to know. Because until we know where we're at, we can never get to where we want to be. And even if we are stranded by a military/industrial complex and can't get anywhere anytime soon, I'd still want to know the truth about what is really going on. That's the only way you can start trying to figure out a solution.

If the current approach to existence is morally wrong, based on what endless war entails, then those four words buried in the U.S. Constitution are the most beautiful phrase in the English language.

I don't want to bore you with political science—not now—I'm almost finished with everything I have to say—but I have to tell you this—it's important if you want to know the truth.

America was originally thirteen colonies. The British had us under their thumb, we finally organized, and with help, threw off a long train of abuses and secured freedom. We had the Articles of Confederation and it kept us and our new freedom intact.

Then some people thought some revisions needed to be made, and Alexander Hamilton led a group that went door-to-door to the states selling the idea that it was time to call a convention. Most everyone finally agreed—except Rhode Island, they never made a sale there—and the Founders convened in Philadelphia. After the first few hours they realized they were split in two, between the Federalists and the Anti-Federalists. The Federalists wanted a centralized government. The Anti-Federalists were like, "What?! We just got free from the British! Centralized government?! Just a matter of time before money corrupts, and then what?! Another war for independence?!" Some of the representatives who had shown up turned heel right then and there and left hollering at the top of their lungs that evil was afoot.

The crowd was shocked, but those who stayed hashed things out because there were problems that needed to be solved. After it was written, the Federalists had to go out and sell this new

Constitution to the thirteen states.

When you really want to sell something and it's a tough sale, you have to have solid rebuttals. And the final rebuttal to the Anti-Federalists, who thought it was a mistake to place all that power into three branches of government, was *Federalist 85*. And Hamilton wrote that sales pitch himself. He said—look, if things ever get out of control and Congress becomes so corrupt it's no longer expressing the will of the people—if corruption ever becomes institutionalized—the states can step in, call a convention and purge it. The clause, when satisfied, is *peremptory*, done without debate, and Congress has no option in the matter. That's the essence of the American spirit, that we consent to be governed, and when things go bad we can alter or abolish. That was the rebuttal that made the sale and that's why we ratified the Constitution and became the U.S.A.

The Constitution is the Supreme Law because every other in all fifty states—whether it's about operating a boat off the coast of Maine, or driving a tractor in Texas, or disposing of paint in Oregon—every single law is linked directly to its seven articles and twenty-seven amendments.

Under the authority of Article V, the Constitution says once two-thirds of the states apply, Congress has to issue the call. Just as there *shall be* three branches of government, Congress *shall call* a convention once the applications hit the doorstep. This is the direct language of the law all elected officials of America and members of our U.S. military swear an oath to uphold. In short, the Founders anticipated the political question doctrine way back then and dealt with it directly—that's why the convention call is ministerial in duty, not discretionary.

Now fast forward to the 1960s, 70s, 80s and 90s, when talk of a convention started going around. Look at editorials from those days, "No—not a convention! If a convention happens the Constitution can be torn to pieces! Or maybe a *runaway convention*, and suddenly hundreds of amendments, and everything's a joke!" It's the same argument politicians and the media trot out every time America starts discussing whether or not it's time to call a convention. Not to mention that politics are already a joke, Americans have been conditioned like Pavlov's dog to fear a convention because of what might happen—that it would be some kind of Pandora's box. But what the newspapers and politicians failed to mention is the *ratification* process. They only told us *half the truth*, and as the late great Ben Franklin mentioned, half the truth is often a great lie. The ratification process requires seventy-five percent of the country to agree before anything is added to the Constitution. The Founders knew that to get three-quarters of any group to agree to anything is so difficult that any idea that's even slightly questionable, is toast. It has no chance of being ratified. Only the ideas that are obvious would be ratified. To fear a convention, basically you're fearing a brainstorming session—the very thing that has to happen for any hope of survival. The Founders knew then what we know now, that governments can become corrupt, and that's why the legal mechanism of the convention clause was placed in the Constitution. It's King Kong sitting there to keep any monsters—corporate or otherwise—from getting between the American people and their government. I mean this stuff isn't rocket science or anything.

So, if Article V was supposed to be the mechanism to save the day when things got corrupt, then why are things the way they are? And there's an answer. In order for there to be a *convention for proposing amendments*—those are the four words—there has to be applications from two-thirds of the states—and the reason we're living under a cap of disinformation called the military/

industrial complex, and the reason there's no health care or an education for whoever wants it, is because there are over five hundred applications requesting a convention and Congress has never called it. All the state applications are there right now in the Congressional Record, and one Congress after the next ignores them. *Laches* it's known as legally—ignoring something on purpose.

So the truth that we're not allowed to talk about is that besides those who no longer care, whether you know it or not, we're all either Conventionists or Anti-Conventionists—you're either for a convention and open discussion or you're not, and if you're *against* a convention you're either ignorant, in denial, or part of the problem. And because the problem is causing the levels of misery in the world that it is—so a few can benefit at the expense of the many—makes it a moral dilemma. Thoreau already said it all in *Civil Disobedience*. If a government turns you into an agent of injustice, and taking a moral stand means ending up in jail, then sometimes the only place for a just person *is* jail. When we refuse allegiance, the revolution is accomplished—and what I really wanted to get across to you is that a convention is a *peaceful revolution*. The Declaration of Independence was written into the Constitution—that's why it's so *great*—that's the genius of it—because it provides for peaceful revolution.

Anyway, we're trapped by whatever forces control banks and corporations. And if we need to get out from underneath that, an Article V Convention is the way to do it. I'm not saying we should all be out on the corner with a banner and a bullhorn foaming at the mouth about it, but we should at least know what ought to be done. Isn't that important at least? To be aware of what *ought* to be happening? The way you see things affects the way things look. I mean at the very least we should be making it the butt of jokes—the bathroom is out of toilet paper—someone call a convention!

I'm a dreamer, I know, but imagine this—Congress issues the call to the states with a date to convene. The states hold special elections for delegates, and before long we'd start getting the human interest stories of who these Americans are, and what they wanted to propose. Then they'd fly to the Capitol and the gavel would fall, calling the convention to order. On live TV we'd get to watch the delegates propose ideas—the good, the bad, and the ugly—and in the process a few modern-day Jeffersons and Madisons would emerge. They'd be on the news and late-night TV just like senators are today. Then after all the ideas were proposed, the gavel would fall again, end the convention, and everyone would go home. Then we'd start getting the stories about which states had approved which ideas, and as soon as any one of them reached the thirty-eight–state threshold—boom— ratification. Think about what that process would do to the political landscape. It would be amazing. It would be a peaceful revolution.

Whenever you debate an Anti-Conventionist though, and they give the same bogus reasons—that the whole Constitution can be torn up—which is a lie—so they can remain in denial— ask them why it's there? Why is the provision for a convention there in the first place? And because all the applications are on record, it's a constitutional requirement a convention be called— so to be an Anti-Conventionist today is actually to be *Anti-Constitutionalist*.

But just ask an Anti-Conventionist why—why is the convention clause in the Constitution in the first place? They don't like it.

21

That's pretty much it. To pull it together I'd start with what the Sumerian tablets say. And about how the *missing link* hasn't been found and never will be because it doesn't exist. For millions of years we were just naked apes—no specialized tools, no fire, no art. And then as if out of nowhere we *Homo sapiens* arrived on the scene. Almost every field of the humanities points to somewhere in the not-too-distant past where something occurred that quite accurately can be described as a *creation*. And it turns out that *art* is the thing that marks that change in consciousness—art in the sense that we began to depict ourselves or aspects of our existence on cave walls.

The two words that distinguish the divide between our mind before we made art and our mind after, also happen to be the two words that expose the divide between humans and all the other animals—*Sentience* and *Sapience*.

Sentience is intelligence with the ability to sense and feel. *Sapience* is the same ability, but in addition to that, the ability to *reflect* on sensations and feelings—in other words—the ability to *know*. Animal consciousness can take a stick and get ants out of a hole, and we can too, but we can hold the stick up and look at the ants and wonder about them and ourselves and everything else. And once you start to wonder, if you have the time, you naturally start looking for answers.

What about elephants and gorillas who paint, aren't they sapient? Elephants and gorillas don't attempt to leave a record of their existence out in the wild. If you go to public forums on the Internet—science forums—you see the same argument over and over. You tell all the stuff about sentience and sapience, and the pre-art and art-capable mind, and they say things like, "Well, beavers build dams—how do I know they're not leaving them as monuments to their existence?" Or, "Well, maybe Neanderthals had a habit of erasing the art they made." Look, beavers are not leaving dams as monuments, and Neanderthals never attempted to record their existence with art. And no, your dog or cat is not secretly trying to figure out how to use your ATM so they can sneak down to the pet store. And every year there are news reports in the papers about some scientist who has done a study on this or that, or has found this or that out in the field, but in the end it's true—no creature before our kind made art and none had language made up of symbols.

Another thing about that anthropology class, and Levy-Bruhl, and how primitives could see something as A and *not* A—that a tree can be a tree and something else at the same time—I remember the professor mentioned something about a tribe in Africa, and how they would stick their spear point into the track of an animal, hoping to affect the success of the hunt. Or sometimes they'd stick it in the footprint of a tribe member, hoping it would make them sick or die or something. And I thought about it. And I wondered, what are they doing? And the answer is, they're taking deliberate action in hopes of causing things to turn out the way they want them to. Based on desire, they're executing the whims and designs of their imagination onto life. We stand in line at the market today, thinking about what we can do to make things go the way we want. It's not that we have a civilized mind and people thousands of years ago didn't, it's just that we have more ideas in our heads about what existence is. Instead of a spear, we have e-mail and cell phones. But most of us are still the same primitives we've always been, which is why it's true that people interested in *ideas* are above average—because the less you know the more primitive you are.

Whether you're inclined to seek out ideas or not—no matter who you are—even if you're President of the United States—it's hard to know what to think about ourselves. We all know what it's like to be absorbed in a phone conversation, or to drive a car mindlessly, but when we get off the phone, or our off-ramp comes up—or we realize we just missed our off-ramp because we were on the phone—we land back in our bodies. Where were we? We don't know how to explain what happens when we do that.

If it really was another race of beings who look like us, like it says in the Bible, and they were the ones who engineered us, then you have to go to the story of God and the Serpent—Enlil and Enki—in the garden—right there where the Tigris and Euphrates Rivers meet. Enlil said No, that we were to remain dogs to the gods, and they weren't going to tell us we're as great as them—that we're sapient—cradles of consciousness—just like them. That's why Enki told Eve it was a lie, that she wouldn't die if she took a bite. And she went to Adam and said, "Guess what?"

"What?"

"That fruit from that tree we're not supposed to eat from?"

"Yeah?"

"One of the gods gave me some and told me I wouldn't die if I ate it."

"Did you eat it?!"

"Yeah."

"And you're not dead?"

"No."

"Here, let me try—does it taste good?"

*

I always wondered what the Eos and Tithonous myth meant, of a goddess falling in love with a mortal and wanting to spend eternity with him. I used to think it was somehow a metaphor for life itself. That we're not meant to have immortality, because if we did we could never know the things you can only know when you're mortal.

If you place the myth alongside what the cuneiform tells, then all it means is that the gods lusted after us. Jung was wrong when he said the gods of old have become diseases today. The gods didn't become diseases, the gods were diseased—with desire—just like us. Just like any sapient creature can be. As soon as you start to desire you're in for trouble, which in a nutshell is basically everything the Buddha and all the Zen monks who followed have ever said. Except for those of us free of desire, the rest of us are children.

But if the gods are real and full of desire like us, I've always wondered if we can become gods to the gods. Everything you need to know about living and walking as a god is in *The Meditations* by Marcus Aurelius. The Stoic philosophy—like, when you're working and have a job to do, do it the best you can, and don't act like it's tougher than it is, or if it's a cool job, don't get all vain about it—and don't make fun when someone says a word or a phase the wrong way—and if someone does something wrong, let the wrong stay where the wrong was done—and if someone tries to make amends for an offence, accept it—don't go around finding fault—and with everything else, look to what *ought* to be done, and not the reputation to be gained. Act with gravity, without affectation, and don't let anything foul your ability to control what you yourself say and do. That's being a God.

Oh, and cover your mouth when you yawn, people seem so much less a god when they don't.

*

Something else was—that in the same way as we have eyes, ears, and noses, the archetypes are common, universal features of our minds. And not only are they nodes of psychic energy that manifest in our stories—the knight who slays the dragon, Luke Skywalker, Batman, Spiderman—but because history is replete with acts of human heroism, that means archetypes are manifest in our instinct too—in our biology. In that way, an archetype is the thing that joins the psychic world and the physical world—the big *inside* with the big *outside*. Man is the bridge between spirit and nature because archetypes are the bridge between mind and matter.

I had thought I came up with the idea, but Emerson saw it first! All of nature—the planet, the stars, the universe—is metaphor for the human mind. I think there's more to say about this, but I haven't turned it over enough yet. Maybe next time.

But it's all a big metaphorical dream. The best example—of course—is surfing. Because the wave lines up before us the same as dates and events in our lives do, and we surf on down the line as best we can. Some people are really good surfers. They can get totally deep in the barrel and carve weightless—they're good at setting up parties, or good at knowing when someone needs a nudge in one way or another, or to be left alone, or maybe even left behind. Maybe the human heart is just a surfboard. And when you go too far with one way of thinking—either the mystical or the rational—is when you tend to wipe out. You have to be able to surf between the two.

Whatever life is, the meaning of it is pretty simple—that in order to be good at something you have to practice, and if you want the type of happiness that really satisfies and lasts, you have to set up goals and work to achieve them.

All the screwing up I did in my past, not being strong and quitting pot and all that stuff—I'm not going to preach and say you should never smoke pot—all I can say is that I really shouldn't have been smoking it as much as I was, and my heart was telling me not to, and I didn't listen, and I made things really difficult for myself.

I was getting screwed up as much as I was because I had some self-esteem problems. But I've worked on it. So if you're like me, I can tell you, there's hope things can change. When things get tough you've just got to hang in there, and don't complicate things by getting stoned all the time.

That's pretty much everything. That, and if America held a national convention, we might be able to right the wrongs that have gone on in this country since we took it from the Native Americans, and that maybe it would lead to world peace.

The Hopi Indians have a prophecy. It says that if mankind does not become peaceable and blend with the land, that we'll *cause* a catastrophe. In other words, their prophecy is saying that the hearts and actions of mankind affect physical reality—which boiled down, is everything Jung and a lot of modern physics say.

What we do and how we think and what we say affects how things unfold here on Earth. That's why the Bible and every other religion, in one way or another, teaches the same thing—that in the beginning there was the *word* and the *word* was God. Words are pieces of God and we speak them—that's why they say God sits on the tip of your tongue. *God is Consciousness*, and it's scary but the truth is, *we're gods*. Most people would rather put God somewhere up there, in heaven or someplace. If they do that, they won't feel as responsible for the only thing they can control—themselves. They want to think it's somewhere outside, instead of inside, where it was in the beginning and will be till the end. Who wants to accept the responsibility of being a god? Sometimes it's terrifying, but when you're special—and we are—you just have to deal with it.

＊

Why am I sitting in your bar here off 52nd—drinking beer in the middle of the day—as the clever hopes of a low and dishonest decade expire? You really want to hear it? You've been a great listener by the way—glad it hasn't been busy. A lot of the time the story you're telling—it's who you're telling it to that makes all the difference. Thank you for listening.

22

When I went off on a political tangent, talking Article V and politics all the time, after a while, today—when we're not allowed to talk about the truth—naturally I became a burden to everyone I knew. A total drag. I've heard a friend's wife sigh the sigh of burden knowing I was going to be at his place for a while. To be *that* is the lowest point you can get in life. The only good thing about it is that you can't go anywhere but up.

Right around then—when I was making everyone I know puke—I was crazy about this one supermodel. She was my muse. And she lived in Malibu too. In *People* I saw pictures of her coming out of the market at Trancas, and I'd read a few interviews and found out she was into Buddhism and yoga, and I was totally crazy about her. When a magazine with her on the cover came out, I'd get it and get all inspired to write stuff. I even kept a copy of collected poems in my jeep in case I ever ran into her. But then the magazines announced she got married to a famous actor, and then I didn't have a muse. I was officially without a muse. I was museless for a while.

Right around then, I was getting serious about art again. Like I said, I've always gone and got art supplies and painted and stuff, but three years ago I was experimenting with oil pastel and gouache. I developed this technique where you can make abstract stuff that's pretty cool to look at. You just capture the space with some oil pastel, and then paint gouache over it. Then if you want, after it dries, you can take a palette knife, scrape away the pastel, and with some running water rinse away all the gouache. It's almost like developing a photo the way it emerges when it's finished. I have a whole essay about what the art theorist Arnheim says and what the color theorist Luscher says and what I'm trying to do. The ones that turn out really good you can sell for a few bucks out of coffee shops and restaurants.

But I was all bummed about being alone and museless, and that I wished I would've just kept my mouth shut about politics. Then one night I walked into a movie theater to see a comedy. I was so depressed, I had to get a laugh.

The movie starts, and it's about a loser. The opening shot is the guy coming home to a zero on his phone machine. It made me even more depressed and I was going to walk out, but then the love interest was revealed. And there she was, the most beautiful thing in the world. This actress that just struck me dumb. The sight of her made my head bobble like I was dizzy. A physical sensation swept my body. I'm pretty sure I levitated. And it wasn't just her looks, her voice, her laugh, I was just captivated in a way I never had been before. If there was a woman that beautiful on the face of the planet, how could anything be bad?

After the movie I stopped at a bookstore, and at the register they had this tray of charms. Just little pictures of angels and bodhisattvas, things you could attach to your key ring. I got this one of a Buddha in the lotus position. It was colored yellow, orange, pink and green. I usually don't get stuff like that, but I guess I was so happy about the possibility of a muse after having been without one for so long.

The next day I went on the Internet to find out what I could. Turns out she'd done a couple small films and a little TV. I looked everywhere to see if she was married or not, but no luck. I did find a brief interview where she used the word *consciousness*, which made me even more crazy about her.

I printed up a picture I found. She was not just another muse in a long line of muses—the thoughts and feelings of her made me want to accomplish something great, to get serious about things. It was a feeling I'd never had before. I'd always been this kind of fool, dreamily floating through life, but she made me want to come down and make something of myself. I mean the other muses—sure I'd be happy to meet up and try and kiss them and stuff, but they never had me motivated to gain recognition in the real world.

Then one night after doing art and drinking beer, I went looking for a new picture of her and I found a list-serve of her fans who would post messages about when she was going to guest role in a TV series or something. I read all the posts and then posted a poem saying I was a poet and artist and she was my muse.

A little while later, I sent her agent my script about the Ghost Lady and the Drifter, but never got a reply. After that, for like two years, whenever a new poem came along, I posted it. But then one night I got all buzzed on beer and posted a really lame one, with politics and all. Well—that was it—to anyone on the list paying attention, I was a *kook*. And there were like fifty anonymous e-mails on the list, and I was always sure she was actually one of them, keeping an eye on what her fans were saying—or to see if there were any kooks like me all crazy about her.

So now I was that guy, the kook who'd never have a chance with her. Even if she'd secretly liked any of the poems, after that one post, the chance of being able to capitalize on anything was over. I kept posting poems anyway. And for like more than a whole year, no one posted anything. And then one day someone posted a message saying she was in a play here in New York City. Without even knowing where I'd get the money, I replied to the list that I was going to see the play and asked if anyone else wanted to meet up for a show. From that I got an anonymous e-mail from some guy saying he'd read my posts over the months, and that if I was a whack-job and scared or upset her in any way he was going to hunt me down and make me sorry. I replied saying, "Dude, I'm just an artist, she's my muse." He didn't respond.

Because it was possible she subscribed to the group, or someone she knew did, I wrote a letter to her and posted it.

I wrote that I was coming to her play, that I was a fellow artist, she'd been my muse for a while, and even though she didn't know it, she'd already inspired art.

I told her how I'd been graced with girlfriends over the years, but had never been struck dumb the way I was with her.

I told her I had some stuff hanging up in a sushi bar down by Zuma Beach and mentioned that if she was ever there to stop in, and if she liked one she could have it. And then I told stuff about Jung's quote, "Man lives in psyche," and how we're all living a collective dream, and how I had some coincidences involving her, and how I knew enough to know that even though the psyche is such a powerful thing as to attract situations into an individual's reality, it's folly to base life decisions on such. And even though I'd be the first to admit I'm a dreamer, I was practical too. And that I was a bit of a salesman. And that I had a sales pitch for her.

I told her that the manifestation of her soul inspired mine to create—poetry, painting, sculpture, plays, scripts, prose. And how that's one of the ways humanity works—a muse inspires an artist to create. And how everything is beautiful and perfect—yes sometimes sad—but beautiful and perfect—the frown, the smile, the paradox of it all. The greatest truth is that there is no greatest truth.

I said OK, so I'm a dreamer and you're my muse, so what— get in line with all the other dreamers, right? And how I would, and how just as a fan I'd be happy to meet her on that level alone, but that I'd be crazy not to attempt to persuade her to meet with me. I told her if we met up and talked about plays for a few minutes she might spark a new one. I told her nothing's for sure, but it might be a sweet episode in the grand scheme of things. I told her if I didn't hear from her I wished her success and all the best, because she really was such a bright light.

This was last year, and I'd never been—I was just blown away. I got here and walked around, went to places Holden talks about in *Catcher*. I visited Hell Gate Bridge where John Diabo got in the way of himself. Down on Mercer Street I saw a blown-up photo of Edie in a window. New York City is amazing, and I'm walking around thinking I could live here—that I'd trade the Pacific Ocean for my muse.

The night of the play I asked the usher if the actors exit out the front and if it's OK to say Hi and wish them success as they leave. He said people do it all the time.

I go in, watch the play, and she's awesome—just a great artist. She plays her part perfectly. I'm starting to get butterflies, won- dering if I'm going to be able to pull it off, or if I was just going to freeze up to the point where she'd go something like, "Oh, that's so sweet of you to come. Thank you, good-night, and have a nice life."

The play ends, the cast comes out and takes their bows. She's just incredible.

I go out front, and ten or fifteen people are there, and before long a couple of the actors come out dressed in their street clothes. We thank them for a great performance and they leave. After about a half-hour the whole cast had come out and gone—everyone but her. And I just started to get the worst feeling that she'd read my letter on the list-serve and left through the back or something. The usher and the ticket window lady are getting ready to lock things up. They know my story, I told them about how I wanted to say Hi and wish her well. Finally the usher says he'll go check to see if she's still in the building, he opens the door, and there she is. She's with two companions, an attractive woman, obviously her mom, and a young girl.

"Oh my gosh! Hi!" I said. "I thought you were great tonight!"

"Well thanks!" she said. She was even more beautiful in person. I kind of froze. Nothing was forming, just completely flustered, and then, before the silence became uncomfortable, I blurted, "Your beauty is an inspiration!" And she was like, "Wow! Thank you!"

"I'm a writer and I want to write a play for you!"

"Wow—that's great!"

"Would it be all right if we met for a couple minutes before your matinee tomorrow? Just—ya know—to ask some general questions about your favorites—maybe some historical figures you find interesting. Just things I can maybe put together in a play?"

"OK," she said.

"Meet you right out front?"

"OK."

"OK," I said, "I'll see you then."

I nodded a good-night, and practically ran out the door and

down the street. Then I go to a bar and it starts to dawn on me that she probably did know about the list, and she probably did like some of my poems, and that she had waited until everyone was gone to meet me. Whether that was actually true or not, I didn't know, but it was a possibility. And thinking about that possibility—that if I would've been more calm—more aware without so much fear—I might've captivated them enough to be invited out. I started to figure that after that, there was no way she was going to meet the next day. She thinks I'm a complete freak now—and she had every reason to!

The next morning I'm shocked about what had happened the night before. I get to the theater, totally nervous, it's late, and in a sense it seemed a relief. It was probably better if she didn't show up, but I turn around and there she is. The look on her face when she sees me is one of dread, clear and unmistakable, like, "Oh great, why did I ever agree to meet this guy." My heart sank. I was like, "Oh hi—thanks for showing up."

"Sure," she said, playing along. But I could tell she wasn't into it.

We headed to this stone bench across from the theater, but it had rained the night before and the whole thing was a puddle with nowhere to sit. There was another bench up some stairs and we headed there. At that point I did the best I could—if I did anything in the following few moments I had with her, I had to convey I was only a fellow artist interested in creating a play—which was true.

"Look," I said, "I saw you had some relatives with you last night."

"Yes, my mom and my niece. They're in town for my niece's birthday."

"I apologize for being so rude and not introducing myself. I just saw you, and my blinders went up, and it was such an extraordinary circumstance—"

"Oh, it's OK," she said. We sat down, I opened a little notebook I had with me, and I started asking a few questions.

"So, what plays do you really like?"

"Oh, I don't know—*Romeo and Juliet*? *The Seagull*, Chekhov? Ibsen's *The Doll House*?" I wrote those down.

"Any period of history you find interesting in particular?"

"No, not really."

"Any historical figure?"

"Maybe Amelia Earhart, Beryl Markham?"

"Oh yeah, *West with the Night*."

"Yeah," she said.

"Well, I don't want you to be late for your play—but look—my flight leaves tomorrow. You want to meet up for lunch or something?"

"Well thank you, but I have to decline. My family is in town, and I do have a man in my life."

"Oh," I said. "Well, I've got some notes here, and that's all I need to try and write a new play."

"That's exciting! Do you normally write plays for people?" she asked.

"No, I'm almost finished with a novel I've been working on forever, and as soon as I'm done I'm working on a play for you. You're my muse."

"Wow!"

"Anyway, I don't want to make you late," I said, and got up to walk her to the theater.

"What's your novel about?" she asked.

"Oh, some derelict surfer in Malibu," I said.

She looked over with a smile, "I bet that's something you might know about, huh?" There's nothing like descending some stairs with your muse, and looking over to see her reply with a smile to something.

"But the protagonist runs into people," I said. "And they turn him on to ideas—have you ever read any Marcus Aurelius?" We're standing at the theater doors, it was grey and blustery, and I'll never forget the way a gust tossed her bangs across her brow.

"Yeah, he's great."

"Wow," I said, "he is great, huh?"

"Yeah."

"Well, thanks for taking a few minutes to chat."

"Sure."

"After I finish the novel—who knows—maybe I'll be able to write something."

"That's so cool!"

"Well, have a good play."

"And you have a safe flight back to LA!" We said good-bye and I walked away relieved I'd averted a major disaster compared to how things could have gone.

So there I was, back in a cab, so stoked I'd just talked with my muse, and glad I left her with a nice feeling, but getting out, I go to get money for the fare, and there in my pocket is the charm from the night I found out about her. I'd forgotten to give it to her!

I jumped into a cafe and started composing a note. And I had to do it quick—it absolutely had to be there before she finished her matinee.

I thanked her for sitting and talking with me and said I thought she was the most beautiful thing in the world. I told her that back when I found out about her I'd bought something and forgot to give it to her. I told her that of course I wanted to meet with her again, though she'd mentioned there was someone in her life. I said, knowing life, we know you never know what tomorrow will bring. I told her that if things ever changed between her and whoever it was she was with, that we should meet up. I told her we both knew about Marcus Aurelius for starters, and that I'd love to show her a good time.

About the enclosed charm, I told her that if it looked nice attached to a present for her niece, to feel free to add it. I taped it to the bottom of the note and got it back to the theater just in time. I hand it to the usher, the same tall, old black guy as the night before, and he told me it would get to her.

I got back to California, and within a day I decided I needed to overnight a few chapters of my novel and some poems to show I was sincere, that I was serious about writing her a play.

In a note to her agent I asked if she'd tell her the guy she met with had sent something, and that if she seemed disinterested, or there had been a bad experience in the past, to just drop it in the mail unopened and I'd get the message.

In the letter, I told her the last thing I wanted to be was another guy she was kind enough to spend a few moments with, turned into a pest. I told her I understood that some guy telling her that she was his muse was not the most reassuring sign of sanity, but that I was a poet, artist, and a man, and in order to roll the boulders of creation, sometimes I needed inspiration. That that's the way it's always been with poets and artists. I told her I had no idea how many guys had written her, I was just a person and she was my muse. I told her I wanted to tell her other things about myself and my life, but that it would be inappropriate right then. I told her the enclosed chapters of the novel and poems were supposed to be evidence of talent. I thought there might be some possibility that if she read everything, she'd recognize me as someone she wanted to know, or if she ever broke up with her boyfriend and we ran into each other again, she'd remember me.

I never heard back, and for about the last year I've been writing my ass off to finish the novel. And then, about a month ago, someone posted that she was in another play—which meant that in order for me to go see her, I had to be able to say I finished the novel, and was working on something for her. So I burned the midnight oil every night for the last month, and I did it. I finished the novel—last week. It's a first draft and all—it'll be revised—but I finished it. I'd like to think it stands on its own.

Then the same thing, I posted I was going to see her and if anyone wanted to meet up for a matinee to let me know. And I got here and saw her last night.

The same thing as before too, the play was great, she was great. But after it was over, this time, in this cramped space, besides about twenty other people, there were about five guys trying to talk to her and get her autograph. Two of them had flowers for her. I wanted to see if she even recognized me.

After watching her be very gracious to three or four guys trying to score points, she started to make her way out, and as she approached she recognized me, and came right up and gave me a hug.

"How are you?!" she asked.

"Good!" I said. "You were great tonight!"

"Thank you!"

"Hey guess what?!"

"What?!"

"I finished the novel!"

"Congratulations!"

"That means I'm writing you a play now!"

"Wow—that's fantastic!"

"Say—what are you doing tomorrow—you want to meet up for some coffee?!" She hesitated, and in her eyes I saw a recognition. I saw her recognize that I thought something might happen between us, though she knew it never would. She made sure what she was going to say wasn't overheard. She stepped to the side over from the door and repositioned us.

"Jack," she said. "I'm not sure you understand."

"What?"

"I'm really glad to hear about you finishing your book, and maybe the play will be great, but I want you to know, I'm in love with someone."

"Oh."

"I apologize if I'm presuming anything, but I've had some experiences in the past. I want you to know I'm planning on spending the rest of my life with someone."

"Not me."

"Oh—don't take it like that!" she said with a big, huge beautiful smile. "Things will happen! You'll find your someone!"

"Yeah, I just wanted it to be you."

"No, you *thought* you wanted it to be me—you just haven't found out yet who you're *supposed* to be with!"

It's all ridiculous in a way, but maybe in another life it will turn out exactly how the poet or artist imagines it. They write and paint and live with their muse.

Now I get to learn the hardest lesson of the Stoics, accepting the life given—that she's not sitting here beside me—that we're not going to be falling asleep next to each other tonight. I don't know how long it's going to take to get over it. Probably never. I really, *really* wanted it to be her.